ABSOLUTION

BOOK TWO: A FAMILIAR GROTESQUE

I0607815

R.M. SEAN BENJAMIN JAFFE

www.EschatonMedia.com

DEDICATED TO THE ONES I LOST
AND THE ONE WHO STAYED.

This is not how you planned it, Not the life you had in mind
Winding days have spiraled into years, And the past is long resigned

Serenade the shade and shadow, Cry a tune for days gone by
Scream a song for all you lost along the way- And the one you left behind

After all the words unspoken, After all the deeds undone
In the dark, where certainties are few, And your song is still unsung

Celebrate the hour of madness, Ride the wave that turns the tide
Dream a song for all you lost along the way... And the one you'll never find

Is it too late for a new day? Is it too late to cross the line?
Is it too late for a new way? Shine down the light...
   -Guilt Machine, "Leland Street"

MONDAY

"I always had a repulsive need to be something more than human. I felt very puny as a human. I thought, "Fuck that. I want to be a superhuman."

- David Bowie, Fas Ferox - A Modern Day Mythology - World Walkthrough (2006)

I rubbed my temples as she asked me all of the questions on the list.

" Full name?"

" Michael Daghlivan."

Amanda Peters' office is a drab affair of beige and that pale municipal olive drab that government files are required to be kept in. Papers stack high and ragged on the desk made of chipped and orange-grey wood that clearly used to serve in a forgotten school district before it came here.

" Former Name?"

" Cage. Michael Cage."

" And your former affiliation?"

" Society Blood. Lictor to the Atlantic City, Philadelphia, and New York Regional courts."

The centerpiece of the office decor, however, is a rusty six-gun mounted in a plaque on the wall. According to Amanda Peters, it belonged to the legendary Jesse James. If you get her drunk enough without her (now ex-) husband around, and she'll tell you the story of how she won it in a particularly rowdy blowjob contest with three other girls in the Two-Bit Saloon in St. Joseph, Missouri, about four weeks before he was shot down. She met her husband Nielsen about a

6

year later, an eccentric, wealthy tinhorn from out East who'd swept her off her feet with his charm and his money, saved her from the life of a hooker, and ultimately, from mortality itself.

" And your current age? Estimate if you have to."

" One hundred and twenty one."

She folded her clipboard against her chest.

" Why, Mr. Daghlian, you're just a baby."

I smiled at her gently mocking condescension. Despite what our HR department wants us to believe, it's never completely comfortable when one Reintegration Rep counsels another. For me, there was always a tacit implication of inferior and superior that sat poorly with the male alpha-brain, an acknowledgement that we were all holding on by our fingertips but the one in the big chair had a slightly better grip than you.

Or maybe it was just me.

And it was that much worse because I was starting to slip so very, very badly.

" So, Michael Daghlian, what do you want to talk to me about?"

" I've been drinking. A lot."

She nodded knowingly as I tried to sink deeper into the couch. I was stonewalling. The drinking had been going on for years.

Ten years ago I took my first breath in nearly three quarters of a century. Within hours, I had found the woman I had waited my entire undeath for, Laura Shephard, my fiancee. Thanks to a curse placed by the controlling psychopath that created me, she hadn't aged a bit since the day I was turned, but she had been doomed to fall into a coma from the second the sun dipped below the horizon until the next day. We were married within the year, and I had taken work with the Department for Post-Blooded Rehabilitation- the agency where I was now. We lived in a house in downtown Jersey City, a short walk from the commuter train that took me to my office and her to the various galleries where she exhibited her paintings. It was the ideal way to finally grow old together.

That was the plan.

" So, the drinking.... Do you drink alone?"

" Sometimes. I remember some of my victims. I remember the dead

7

faces, you know? Pale, with that stupid expression they all had that always seemed to say ' This is the last goddamned thing I expected to happen to me when I got up this morning....' "

The plan.

A week or so ago a Post-Blooded, one of my cases, actually, was shot to death in Queens. Croglin Grange, the Vampire, had been Majordomo to Prefect Walker Jericho of New York City for almost twenty years. When the redemption came, Croglin Grange became Vernon Granger and did his best to fade away quietly. He was mugged and shot outside his apartment.

I got to see him in that bed, bleeding out, so pathetic. So human. Like most humans, he died forgotten and alone.

And then there was Laura. A few days later, I found her fucking a stranger in our house, and while I was somewhat startled by it, our prior conditions precluded monogamy a long time ago. This tryst was different, clandestine, and it was clear I wasn't supposed to know about it. This bothered me, I guess, but I was much more dismayed to find myself feeling nothing at all.

Or so I thought.

Two days ago, I caught and tortured a petty thief in a Herald Square convenience store. I mean... I really tortured him. I knocked the gun from his hand and sliced his lips off with a razor blade. I went back to work as though nothing happened, and so far I haven't heard a thing about it. That night, I went downstairs to find Croglin Grange in my backyard babbling about how he had faked his death and he had rediscovered the blood...

Only no one was actually there.

I toyed with a pamphlet on her table entitled "OLD CRAVINGS?" I opened to a paragraph heading in bold letters: HALLUCINATIONS AND VOICES: WARNING SIGNS.

" Michael?"

I blinked. " Yeah. Sorry." I folded the pamphlet and put it in my lap.

Granger was dead. He hadn't faked an goddamned thing. I had hallucinated the whole thing, fired three shots into my neighbor's backyard. Laura cooked up some story of a prowler for the cops as I sat in the kitchen nursing a bottle of Jack and staring into the middle distance. She closed the door as they turned away, walked past me, gave me a look one might give a homeless man or an infection, shook her head, and wordlessly went to bed.

I looked down at the glossy trifold.

If you suffer hallucinations or hear voices encouraging you to drink human blood, you are a high risk for Recidivism. Contact a D.P.B.R. Rep immediately. Don't put yourself or the people you love in danger. Call today!

I folded it up and blinked.

" Michael? Does your wife know about your drinking?"

I nodded, and lied. " She's the reason I'm here. I think I just need regular sessions with a regular shrink, Amanda. I used to party pretty hard back in the day, and ... you know, I don't think this body can handle it."

" That makes some sense. Still, I think we should talk..."

I sat up straight.

" Sure. Sure... As long as you're buying lunch, we can go down for Korean."

" I'm buying as long as you're gonna cover for me Wednesday."

I nodded. She smiled and regarded her charts.

" You know I have to ask the questions."

I nodded and grinned, preparing another barrage of lies.

" Experienced any homicidal or predatory urges in the past month?"

I sliced a man's face open because he interfered with my lunchtime schedule.

" Nope, unless you count Holland Tunnel Traffic."

She chuckled. " Do you regularly get a full night's sleep?"

Not in a week. Not a wink.

" Like a baby."

" Have you experience visual or auditory hallucinations ?"

Experienced one? I had a conversation with one and shot it in the face.

" Nope."

" Have you attended any Coven or Bloodline meetings ?"

Does this count?

" Does this count, Amanda?"

She smirked a conspiratorial grin at me that in that half second made me consider trying to fuck her on the desk.

" Finally- Have you followed or stalked individuals of a savory nature ?"

Give me time.

" I don't have time to follow myself, these days. I'll see you in a few days. I'm gonna try and just get rid of all the booze in the house, for starters. I'm just trying to be proactive, you know."

She nodded. " Good. Good instincts. If more of us thought like you did there wouldn't be a problem, Daghlian. Seriously, though, are you still covering the support group for me on Wednesday? I have a *date*."

Her eyes barely held back the pain of saying that again after having been married for a century.

I nodded and rubbed my temples, dying to get out of her office forever. Too much truth. Too much admission. I'm not prepared to admit any of this to myself ever again.

* * * *

It was a nice night. Atlantic City in September was hazy and cool, but the bitter ocean cold of fall hadn't yet blown in. The sounds of celebration were everywhere, and most houses had a streamer or two, or at least a flag out in front. The salty tang of summer's end hung bitter and smoky over the dull reds and browns of the brick and stone, but the view of the beach at night still promised a few good times before the freeze came.

Michael left his apartment to find a paper on his stoop loudly announcing the surrender of the Japanese. He had immediately headed down to the Traymore to celebrate. About three Gin & Tonics in, he met Jewel, a WAC file clerk from Pittsburgh that had similar ideas about exactly how to celebrate victory in the Pacific. They shared a liberally poured Manhattan and headed back to his walkup on St. James' Place. There, he got even drunker on the alcohol already in her bloodstream, being sloppy but careful to have left her just enough blood in her system to push back as he took her, dizzy and confused, from behind.

10

She grasped blindly at the covers on the top of the bed, head down, backside raised, a spill of strawberry curls bouncing against her shoulders with each thrust. Michael, behind her, watched half-mesmerized by the ripples of flesh against her thighs and backside as he slammed into her. Pulling back, he looked down at his hardness drawing back wet and shiny from her parted lips, and made sure to maintain pressure on the shoulder where she'd been bitten lest her raised heart rate squirt sanguine all over the bedspread. He'd learned it was like giving a shot to someone who was phobic of needles. Distract them with another sensation and they rarely even notice they've been wounded.

" You look like you're having fun."

He blinked and looked up. He'd probably have been more surprised if he weren't drunk, but he was, and unexpected visitors at any time weren't something he was unacquainted with. Seated in a comfortable red leather chair opposite the bed was Jasmine Bhaterjee. She was a tall, sultry vampiress of some now-extinct Southeast Asian stock, mocha-skinned with red hair and a light dusting of freckles across her face. She had been an assassin since since she was twelve, which Michael estimated based on their numerous conversations together to be sometime around the birth of Christ. She lounged, dressed in expensive silks and reading the paper as though she was on the subway. Looking up at him with bright, languid, kohl-rimmed eyes she smiled a fanged smile.

" Don't let me stop you. Carry on," she intoned through an Indian accent with a vapor of British inflection. Michael felt his cock jump just hearing her. She'd always been the one that got away. Jewel clenched on him.

" Mmm..Micuh? Whothefug izzis?" burbled Jewel, not lifting her head from the bed. " Izzat yer fuggin wife, you shit? You married?" If she was offended, it wasn't enough to make her get up, or stop, or indicate in any way that this wasn't ideal.

Michael placed a hand flat on her back, as if to quiet her.

" Jasmine? You... uh... you want in?"

" No. But it was rude of me to interrupt." She waved dismissively at Jewel. " I'm his... uh... roommate. Ignore me."

" Oh, OK." Jewel got up on her elbows and pushed back a bit harder. Michael wondered if it was the booze, the blood loss, or some power Jasmine had employed that caused her sudden drop in her already bottomed-out inhibitions.

" So... What brings you here?" smiled Michael, looking down again at what he was doing.

" You killed Leucretia. You killed your Maker."

Michael felt himself go a bit soft as terror splashed into his heart. They were friends, he and Jasmine, but if she'd been hired to...

She gave him a look that quelled his fears.

" Keep your hard-on, I'm not here on her behalf or anything. I wouldn't work for any of her stable of shits and sycophants anyway. I'm here as your friend."

" Oh?"

" Yes."

" What did you need to tell me?"

She sidled up to him and folded the paper.

" I need you to listen. I need you to never, ever forget what I'm about to tell you."

" Sure. You got it." Michael smiled at her, then back down at Jewel's backside.

He didn't actually see Jasmine move.

She was suddenly behind him, blade at his throat, right hand gripping the base of his cock firmly and smoothly. The sensation doubled in him, and he dropped back against Jasmine who caught him and held him up, pulled him out of Jewel's vagina and stroked him twice firmly, causing him to lose all control and send arc after arc of crimson come all over Jewel's back, ass and legs. He shuddered against Jasmine as she stroked him again, gently, drawing out the last drops of his reserve. Jewel collapsed forward, asleep. Michael leaned back, shuddered and prayed that he wasn't somehow drooling.

" What... why... huh..." She had never even so much as touched him before, and they had known each other for over ten years. His knees were weak, and as the orgasm subsided he became acutely aware of the blade. She'd beheaded larger men with less. He'd seen her do it.

" So do I have your attention now, Michael Cage?"

12

" You have my undivided attention."

" Stop celebrating."

She let him go and was quite suddenly, fluidly standing at the side of the bed gently cleaning her hands with a silk handkerchief. The knife was gone. Michael kneeled stupidly before her, naked and cow-eyed.

" ...What?"

" You going to make me repeat myself?" she said, as though disappointed. Michael grabbed his head as though trying to catch it.

" No. No... I... What do you mean, stop celebrating?"

" Stop reveling in your idleness. Do not be one of her brood, Michael. Do not be one of those vampires." She spat the words. " You've been doing nothing but sleeping and feeding for almost two years."

" As... as opposed to?"

" Playing music? Writing poems? Buying stocks, or building a house, or anything?"

" What? Who cares? I'm undead, right?"

She slapped him. He knew it was just to get his attention. If she'd wanted it to hurt, she could have done it in a way that would have shattered his face. If she's wanted him to die, that was also on the table. It was just a slap. He immediately regretted his words.

" You need motivation. You need- and I know it sounds ironic- you need a *life*. You know stories of lurkers in swamps and bogs waylaying travelers? That's what happens when we go crazy out of idleness. Why bother bathing, or living in a house, or anything like that, right?"

Michael swung his feet over the edge of the bed, put them on the floor, and covered his face with his hands.

" It's easy to think that way, Michael, and once you get stuck that way it's hard to stop."

" But I don't want to... just do something so I don't get bored with all the time I have..."

" It's not about that. It's not that your obligations have ceased to be important. You just don't know how to contextualize it against immortality, since you don't yet know what it's like to carry your mistakes for a century or two. I learned that the hard way."

" I don't have any obligations. I'm off the map."

13

" You do. You have obligations all over the place. To yourself, to your art, and to me."

Michael looked at her, framed in moonlight, looking soft and gentle and impossibly old. He wanted her so badly.

" What do you mean, 'You learned that the hard way?' "

She grinned. "You ever hear the story of the *Aswang*?"

Michael shook his head.

" Aswang. It was a Philippino legend of a female vampire who replaced the corpses of her victims with effigies made of wood or vegetation. That was me. I did that for a few centuries while the Vikings were out pillaging Europe. So I fucked off. It was warm down there, and I figured, who the fuck needs clothes or civilization?"

" What happened?"

" I came to my fucking senses when I was stalking this one hut and I heard a mother tell her kids that if they didn't shut up and go to sleep the Aswang would get them. And it was true. That was *exactly* what I was doing. I'd become *that* kind of monster."

Michael looked out the window at the distant beach.

" And we don't do that anymore. If someone becomes that kind of beast, the Society destroys them. And they're right to do it. It's better for everyone."

" Jasmine?"

" Yeah?"

Michael regarded the drenched girl prone before them both. He toweled her off gently, so as to not wake her and make certain that she remembered as much of tonight as possible as a drunken fever dream.

" That... had to be... the single sexiest thing anyone has ever done."

" Did I get your attention?"

Michael nodded emphatically.

" Then it worked." Jasmine said, chin up. " There's someone I want you to meet. His name is T'isparigo. He's even older than I am. He'll help you. I'll find you tomorrow and we will go see him. "

Michael looked down.

" Do you want to... get my attention again?"

He turned to her, but she was already gone.

TUESDAY

"Please try to bear with me if the language here is dry, as this is a departure from the sort of papers I normally write for medical journals and scientific ledgers, but I get a great many people asking me questions about what I've learned in my time on the CDC's Post-Blooded task force. Sadly, even after a solid year of study, we still have have almost no answers. The truth is, so much of what they claim they could do is conjecture and hearsay at this point, it's impossible to quantify how much of vampirism was cold scientific fact and how much was legend. However, we do have some baseline facts:

• They existed. That much is unquestionable, given the massive evidence we have gathered, especially in the last days of the purge. Although the Federal Government claims to never have captured and dissected the "Blooded" (as they called themselves) during the Witch hunts, this seems highly unlikely given the nature of the conflict. All documents pertaining to the Federal Government's Witch hunter program are classified, and it's safe to assume they will remain so for quite some time. Regardless, the governments of this and all major nations of the world recognize vampirism as a legitimate phenomenon that ended rather abruptly around the turn of the century.

• They drank blood and gained enormous amounts of caloric energy from what is, genetically speaking, not a terribly nourishing substance. We know that. How they did this, biologically speaking, is unclear and will remain unclear since the strain is technically "redeemed" or genetically extinct.

• They were highly allergic to sunlight, to the degree of instantaneous physical reaction- it was described as "burning" although photographic and video evidence shows no actual

combustion occurred, and accounts reveal activity more like an instant degradation of cellular tissue. This is perhaps the most "normal" of the Vampire's bizarre traits, as there are other diseases, such as cutaneous (erythropoietic) porphyrias, that have similar effects.

• They were also effectively immortal, and possessed massive recuperative abilities. The only other living things possessed of a lifespan rivaling some of the eldest of the Postblooded (Tuthmose Geb Psammeticus, Rebekah Kadi, Comte de St. Germaine, Xanthippe, Na'Qui Kahfi, Cloacina, or Septimus Victor, for example) are plants. A Bristlecone Pine in the white mountains of California was the original record-holder for continuous lifespan at 4700 years old. Tuthmose Geb Psammeticus recalls Predynastic Egypt with some difficulty, meaning he's around five thousand years old. Rumor of a "Maker Mother," a vampire ten thousand years old, remain unfounded. This boggles the mind and turns conventional biology on its ear. Typically, the longest-lived creatures are the least complex, things like plants, molds, and fungus. The Blooded completely subverted this fact for millennia, right under our noses. Even now geneticists and biologists struggle to determine how they did this.

• A genetic virus or prion disease as vampirism seemed to be might be able to act as a catalyst for several "superhuman" mutations, including increased speed, strength, awareness, and other abilities, as well as a massively effective regenerative abilities. After all, these abilities can be chemically induced. However, credibility is strained by some of the other powers these Vampires claimed to have commanded. Mind Control (perhaps through pheromones), Shapeshifting (Perhaps through cell control) and "ESP" (perhaps though enhanced sensory data) are technically possible but seem highly unlikely. Still, the Postblooded insist that they were real.

• The Postblooded claimed to have been in a worldwide "Society" with other, rarer forms of Undead, Werewolves, and even animated inanimate objects. Given the wide amount of diversity and mutation in the Vampire virus, it's assumed that these other creatures were people affected by offshoots of the original virus, if they existed at all. *

*Scientists in Saudi Arabia did find a nest of what they called Ghouls, which certainly differed from the Blooded as we knew them.

17

*The Ghouls were smaller, grey and emaciated, as though arrested in
a later state of decomposition. Unlike the Blooded, they could only
pass for human at a great distance. They exhibited discomfort when
exposed to sunlight, but were not instantly damaged as the Blooded
were, and most startlingly, they ate only rotting meat. Sadly, all
specimens were euthanized in accordance with religious law, and
it is highly unlikely any Ghouls survived the Middle East's rather
extreme reaction to the discovery of the existence of the Undead."*

*• They are universally extinct. Within what must have been a
matter of hours between 12 AM and 12 PM Eastern Standard Time,
January 1, 2000, every single Blooded on Earth was - and I hesitate
to use this word but it fits absurdly well here- miraculously cured,
leaving them perfectly normal human beings, free to commence aging
from the point where their development was arrested as though
nothing had ever happened.*

**-Dr. Thomas Kreitzer M.D., "Myth and Crimson: Unraveling
the Blooded Virus" New York Magazine, June 2001**

I woke up to an unpleasant huffing snort, a disgusting wet sound
that could only be human in origin. Sitting up, I looked into the
bathroom where Laura hunched over the sink, disheveled in robe
and slippers, shivering ever so slightly. There, my porcelain-skinned
angel gripped the edges of the sink and loudly and aggressively tried to
dislodge something from her sinuses before spitting it into the toilet.
Lovely.

" Ugh," she moaned.

" Are you OK?"

" I'm sick." She turned to me, heavy-lidded and half-smiling.
"Remember sick?"

" Not since, aw, jeeze... the Coolidge administration, unless you
count the Change."

" Yeah, well... it sucks."

I realized I still had a primal reaction to her sickness, a revulsion to
it. *No, not that one.* A predator's reaction. I looked down before she
could see my face, but I wasn't sure I was fast enough.

" What... what do you need?" I offered.

18

" This is that strange to you?" She sat up and blew her nose in the rare way that women do when they're not trying to impress anyone. "Chicken soup. Campbells is fine. Just plain old chicken soup."

" You don't want... a doctor or something?"

" It's a day cold, Michael. Chicken soup, maybe some conversation about stuff I hate."

I was already dressed.

" I'm going to see Nigel Huxley today."

" There ya go. A few stories of that pretentious fuck and some Chicken 'N Stars and I'm good."

" You don't like him because he called your work 'immature.' "

" He called my work immature because I'm not a fucking mummy, and I'm not famous enough. And that hypocritical fuckwad just can't wait to splooge all over the newest musician to come out of the gate, yourself included, because you guys throw the best parties. Fuck him."

I nodded and headed down to the car.

At Huxley's massive Union Square apartment, I looked up at his prize Basquiat as I sat on a chair that he'd bought at auction from Max's Kansas City because there was rumor David Bowie had been sick on it at a Diamond Dogs listening party. I'd been at that party and didn't have the heart to tell him that I didn't think Bowie had ever been human, let alone capable of vomiting. But, hey, it did serve to underscore Laura's point.

Since Tammany Hall, Nigel Huxley was as much a part of New York as the smell. He was rich and fancied himself a patron of the arts, and powerful and connected enough that even when the Heretics ran the city they pretty much left him alone. Of all my patients, he was the one that re-acclimated the least, or perhaps simply had never lived any other way. He was rich enough and a big enough contributor to the Department that this never really mattered, though. He had a bad habit of bringing me hallucinogens and designer drugs as a joke when I went to see him, and I'd learned that if I had anything to do that day, I was better off not taking any food or drink from him. Still, I had to occasionally make the cursory attempt to stop by his place and tell him

19

to chill out and he made a point of routinely ignoring me. I lifted the tea he placed before me and stirred it, smelled it, and set it down. He raised an eyebrow, but I kept talking.

" The department says that you never signed the release from that time with the girl from queens. I know you didn't do anything, Hell, I know you're gay, Nigel. But the media watches all of us, and you, you're rich. That's high visibility, now. I have a copy…-"

He sniffed, regarding my reluctance to drink.

" I *also* know how to make it look like I'm eating when I'm not, Michael. You wound me."

I sighed.

" I… I can't. Laura's sick. I want to take care of her, not be a gibbering, shivering burden when I get home, Nigel."

He clinked the spoon on the cup.

" It's just tea, Michael."

I raised my eyebrows incredulously. He nodded to re-enforce his point.

" Seriously?"

" Seriously, just *tea*."

I took a sip. If there was anything in it, I didn't taste it. He looked distant, then smirked.

" Besides, I wouldn't want to get on your bad side, sir."

I put it down.

" What… what do you mean?"

" I know your little secret, Mr. Cage. Everyone makes dirty mistakes… but such a cleanup. I'd underestimated you."

I clenched and looked at him in a way that utterly betrayed that I knew exactly what he was talking about while trying to look like I had no idea what he was talking about. He continued.

" I know you put a boy in the hospital a few days ago, and I know that a series of clinical errors made it so that boy just happened to overdose on morphine in there." He smiled as though I'd fucked a priest. "Dirty, dirty."

My fear gave way to confusion.

" I… I didn't… clean..?"

His face instantly registered understanding.

" Crime of passion, eh? You did put him in there, but didn't take him out. The plot thickens..."

I stood up.

" What the fuck?"

" Am I right?"

" Let's uh... let's say you are. I lost it on a mugger in a bodega a few days ago." I narrowed my eyes at him, to remind him I knew enough about his habits and proclivities to put him in the Castle till his last days, and continued. " I... I never put any hit out him or anything. I don't even know his name. I had no idea what I was going to... going to..."

" Well, looks like someone's got a guardian angel." He smiled.

Was it him? Was he trying to tell me he'd cleaned this up for me, and that we were even? I peered at him as he sipped, smiling, inscrutable.

" Are we done here?"

I put the cup down and nodded. " I'll... fill in the paperwork for you."

" Thanks so much."

A massive weight was lifted from my shoulders. On the ride home, it slowly dawned on my that someone had murdered that kid for me, and that it should bother me more than it had. It was hard to grasp that though the relief, though. I had stopped off at Katz' Deli to get a whole turkey dinner for Laura and carried it gently on the train, concentrating more on trying to somehow psychically keep it warm than the murder of a young criminal on my behalf.

I opened the door gently balancing a huge bag on the crux of my elbow. Ducked into the kitchen, grabbed some wine and the bed tray, and went upstairs to gently place it over her sleeping form. Her rheumy eyes fluttered open. She sniffed and looked up at me, beaming.

" Whuh... whuzzis?"

" Turkey dinner with all the fixin's."

She stretched. " Buh... but.... but..."

I looked hurt.

21

" No, turkey's fine. But, uh, honey, did you get any chicken soup?"

" It's turkey! It's like chicken only better, because it's bigger and makes you sleepy. Also gravy, vegetables, some latkes...."

She nodded and gave me a look like I was a cat that had brought her a headless mouse.

" Thank you, Michael."

" You don't want it?"

" No. No, turkey's good. Thank you, baby. I... I..."

She sniffed and nibbled on the massive drumstick.

" I think... I'm gonna get some more sleep, though, and zap it later, OK?"

I picked up the tray and nodded, and looked back at her, nestled in the bed, so sick and human as she watched me go.

* * * *

Michael Cage sniffed the crisp, cold air and squinted at the Rockefeller courtyard where his protege skated in lazy circles. It was one of those perfect New York Christmas-season nights, wherein a thin, gentle snowfall caressed happy families laden with bags of expensive gifts and the whole thing seemed to have sprung fully formed, like Athena, from the mind of a Madison Avenue ad exec. He leaned heavily against the railing and smiled down at Samantha, who looked up and made a face at him. She continued to make her slow circles as he walked town to meet her by the gateway. By the time he reached the gate, she was there, pulling the skates from her feet. She cocked her head at him as he approached.

He nodded toward her bare feet, eyebrows arched. She returned a look of confusion, trying to discern his expression.

" Oh my, sweetie! Aren't you cold?" He said it less out of concern and more like he was imparting a lesson. She blinked with realization and pulled her boots back on quickly. Taking his arm, they headed up Fifth avenue side by side.

" So, what are you gonna get me?"

" For Christmas? I'm shopping for Laura. I'm gonna find something for you when you're not being so clingy."

" Clingy? Fuck you!" She giggled, and pelted him with a hastily-constructed snowball scooped from the windshield of a parked car as the headed for the train. He laughed.

Underground, the beauty and purity of the snow always gave way to the brown-slick citywater and ragged wet cardboard that seemed to make the trains seem even filthier than usual. They sat below an ad for Johnny Walker on the sparsely-populated train. Samantha frowned. A thin man in a grey overcoat had been staring at her for three stops. She regarded Michael instead.

" You gotta get me two gifts, remember. You owe me for Christmas and next week is my birthday." She peered out the window at the Fulton Street Station, urging the train to move. " Why are we just sitting here? "

Michael sighed.

" Well, what do you want?"

" One of those new cell phone things." She replied.

" What's wrong with your beeper?"

" Cell phone! Cell phone is better! Like a car phone, but, you know, whenever you need it."

" How old are you, again?"

She laid her head against his shoulder.

" I'm twenty-seven. Forever."

" Seriously. Cut the shit."

" I'm 54," she uttered quietly, eyeing a woman of certainly the same age who wore and carried every year in her face.

" You don't feel it."

She shook her head.

" No, I don't."

Across the crowded train, the man crushed her with his stare, and Michael watched him. Samantha was beautiful, and men had noticed on the subway before. She rarely had to say anything more aggressive than "can we help you?" before they scurried off, but something about this one made Michael uneasy.

He stood up to give his line, and his heart froze. The man was staring at him, not her. Something was wrong.

" Can... Can we help...-" he stammered, but the man cocked his

23

head and stared him dead in the eye.

" Stop digging, Michael Cage." The man sat up straight, opening his coat ever so slightly. " Stop digging."

Michael's eyes went wide. He shielded Samantha uselessly with his body, trying to scream to get down, take cover, anything. He managed to blurt out a guttural sound before his ear drums burst and the car went red with fire. He'd seen only the wire, but recognized a bomb.

He was thrown forward into Samantha and blacked out.

Came to.

Screaming, smoke. Samantha shaking him. He tried to understand what she was saying, couldn't. She dropped him and tore out the wrecked door of the subway car. All around, smoke, and smell of burnt hair. He started to hear the moaning and screaming as his right ear drum re-knit. A mother screamed to her injured son. A man called out to his friends, but no one seemed to be dead. It was for him. He could tell the Prefect it was the Heretics, and they'd tell the press it was a terrorist or a drug addict, but it was mean for him.

Michael disappeared in the confusion, running down the tunnel, hot on Samantha's trail. She was running as hard and as fast as she could to keep up with the bomber, and managed to leap for him under a red access light. He pitched forward as she slammed her full body weight between his shoulder blades, rolling with the impact and got to his feet, holding her aloft by her throat. She clawed at his fingers with her inhuman strength and got nowhere.

He turned to Michael still with that fixed stare, and only then did it sink in. The man before him had a hole blown clear through his midsection. He face registered no other emotion than clean contentment, fixed, unmoving. A mannequin. He wasn't human at all.

"What's done is done, Michael Cage. Stop digging."

He dropped Samantha and took off into the tunnels. She rubbed her throat and walked toward Michael, reaching out for him.

" What... what the fuck was that?"

Michael rubbed his eyes.

" It wasn't enough."

WEDNESDAY

"... and that's exactly my point, Christopher. We can no longer trust any single aspect of history. If we were wrong about this, what else don't we really know? Was Lincoln really a vampire? Or Oscar Wilde? Or Christ himself? One must admit, it answers a great many questions. How can we have faith in anything so fleeting as humanity when we can now look back and never once be 100 percent certain that any single figure within it was, in fact, actually human?"

-Neil deGrasse Tyson, "Real Time with Bill Maher" February 2004

I sat between Trencher and Eve Marko. Eve chain-smoked like a fiend, unwilling to give up the once affectation that was now a full-blown addiction, which would likely kill her in a few short years. The wicked irony was that when she was undead, Eve smoked to appear human. Now that she was breathing, it was almost certain to be what would turn her back into a corpse. Trencher, on the other hand, barely breathed. He was one of those shadowy types. I think he spent most of his unlife in hiding and hadn't quite grown out of it. I don't think I'd ever heard him say more than three words at a time.

We sat on uncomfortable folding chairs in Brooklyn's PS 8, in a quiet unused classroom on the first floor. Bright construction-paper flowers smiled at us and reminded us of our ABC's the smeared remains of a lesson remained on the grey chalkboard. I sat with six other former vampires in a small circle, and it was Donovan's turn to speak.

Donovan had been a shapeshifter, and had enjoyed a short stint as a Lictor in Toronto before coming to New York. He now lived out of his car, hung around the local methadone clinic, and sometimes called my office from jail. He wasn't a Recidivist, but he was on the watch list.

"They arrested me for trespassing last week. I was just trying to get into my car. I left some papers I needed in there, you know... when it was impounded, and I needed them for a job i was trying to get at a restaurant. They arrested me, and I didn't break anyone's bones, or nothing, but... I tried. They used a taser on me. They asked if I was Blood, and I said I was a recovering addict, and they let me go. And I was sitting there, just sitting there, in Red Hook... you know... by all the impounded cars? Some have been there so long they got dust that makes 'em look all black- the wheels, the chrome, even the windows. All black and forgotten. And I was thinking, you know, they like *crackheads* better than us. Fucking ...crackheads, man. "

"Yeah. Fuckin' crackheads never ate people. " Marko belched through a cloud of cancer.

" So?"

"SO? Are you fucking kidding me? " She stubbed out the cigarette and immediately lit another, despite my attempt to protest.

" Are all of you motherfuckers so caught up in feeling sorry for yourselves that you don't remember killing and eating people? Because we all fucking did it. We ate people, you damned dirty fuckers. I'm sorry you live in your cars, I'm sorry breathing ain't all it's cracked up to be. But you know what? Back when I was a Heretic, nothing..."

She stood up, clearly just starting in on her rant. This was common. Some rolled their eyes, others looked away.

" Fucking *nothing* pissed me off so much as listening to you gothy little Society Bloods bitch, and fucking whiiine...." She drew out the word for emphasis "... about how you were cursed, and how somehow God was punishing you by making you into blood drinking monsters who flitted among humanity with supernatural powers and everlasting life."

She turned to me, jabbing her cigarette at me for emphasis.

"You know what I think?"

I shrugged at her.

" I think... I think *this* is God punishing us for *that*."

27

She took her seat, puffing angrily. I nodded.

"Well, it's a point of view that certainly makes sense of your two-carton-a-day habit. "

" What is this, fucking Nicotine Anonymous? I thought we were all here to talk about being Post-blooded, bitch."

" Settle down. I didn't mean to insinuate..."

A stocky Egyptian with a shaved head raised his hand. I nodded to him, and looked at the sheet.

"Kun... khoon...?" He cut me off.

" Khunous-hetef. If it's easier, I've used 'Adrian Winslow' for the past several decades," he offered through a barely-audible accent. " I... I have a story I'd like to tell."

I smiled plaintively. "Go ahead, Khunous-hetef."

" I was doing very well as a history teacher, until a student's parents protested and... as you know, they passed the Post-blooded Education Act. "

Donovan gave him a confused look, and he tried to explain.

" Parents do not relish the concept of a vampire, even a human one, teaching their children. The act was passed to preclude Post-blooded from any and all teaching positions save those where we... ahem... teach other Post-blooded."

"This shit again. If we'd listened to the fucking Heretics, we'd at least have a bigger voting bloc."

I moved to shush Eve Marko, but it wasn't her. Jennifer Gitano, a traveling street performer who, to the best of my knowledge, hadn't changed her lifestyle much following her redemption. Khunous-hetef nodded at her.

" Yes, well, I understand. I had two boys in Luxor, and I surely wouldn't have trusted them with something... like me... had I known then. It is, ultimately irrelevant. I tried to publish, but..."

Kuszlieka finally spoke up. "No one was buying."

" No- I know that there was a glut of Post-Blooded memoirs in the early 2000's, but it turned out that I was old enough to be considered despite the manuscript buying freeze. I still remember the Mamluke Sultanate, and I suppose that got their attention. I have about half a manuscript complete, but I am really drawing a blank- seems I can barely remember a single thing that happened in the fifteenth century. It was... most alarming. If any of you were alive then and remember any of it, I could really use a hand."

" I was at Altamont." Donovan offered. Jennifer groaned.

"Altamont? Was that a battle of some kind?" asked the sleepy-looking Egyptian.

Donovan shrugged.

" I guess so, kind of..."

I looked up at the door. A girl- maybe mid-twenties by the look of her- slipped in, trying to look inconspicuous. She looked so much fresher and younger than the rest of us; huge blue eyes behind trendy frames, wavy red hair with pink streaks pulled back into two long pigtails, arms decorated with a fresco of tattoos. She caught my eye and nodded as though caught.

"... But the guy I had fed on was just on so much acid that he crashed his Harley into a dumpster. So I found a stall where I could...-"

I cut him off.

" Sorry to interrupt, Donovan- looks like we have a new arrival."

I looked back at her. "I'm sorry, Amanda's not here this week. Can you tell me your name?"

"Oh, I'm... uh... new. I'm Emily."

The others regarded her warily, predators defending the last scrap of territory they had left due to overwhelming human encroachment.

" Hi, Emily."

" I don't remember you."

Everyone turned to Trencher. His voice was raspy, as though he'd been crying.

" I'd remember you. I remember *everyone*."

" Yeah, I don't remember you either." Jennifer Gitano leaned forward, clutching her bag to her chest. " You sure you're in the right room, kid?"

Emily regarded a folded piece of paper.

" Post-Blooded Meetup and Support group, room 210. This room 210?"

" It is. Are you Post-Blooded?" asked Donovan.

" I don't recognize you," sniped Jennifer.

" Who was the Prefect of London during the War of the Roses?" offered Khounus-Hetef.

" What? I don't know..."

They were turning on her. I tried to regain control.

"Guys, settle down." I said, trying to mitigate the situation.

Gitano jabbed a finger at me.

" No, Michael. You're not Amanda, you don't know. We get one of these a month, some kid coming in here with some bullshit story about how she was boning her own little fanfic Lestat in New Orleans during the reconstruction."

" Prefect Jean-Claude Emmanuelle Bishop," snapped Emily.

" Of London?" asked Khounus-Hetef.

" No," she said. " New Orleans."

" Ahhh, Get the fuck out of here, kid," snarled Gitano. " This isn't about discussing the outfits you and your sexy vampire boyfriend wore to meet the fucking queen of Europe. I sucked a mouthful of pus out of a gypsy with thyroid cancer during World War 1. Write a fucking pretty book about that."

I stood up to regain order, but someone else spoke first.

"Easy, Jenn, " Eve Marko took a long drag off her cigarette, stubbed it out, and lit another. "She was a Heretic. I remember her now."

I didn't like the pallid sneer she offered the newcomer. "Tell them about that."

Emily moved back toward the door.

"No, that's OK. Clearly you guys have... some kind of a thing here..."

I put my hand out, pointing at Eve to keep her damn trap shut. " No. No. Take a seat, Emily. We have Society Blood and Heretic Blood here. It's all moot now anyways. Please." I indicated an empty seat in the semicircle, waved her towards in. Eve giggled.

" Now, go ahead, tell us about who you are and what you did before the Redemption."

" Yeah, Emily. Tell us." I shushed Eve again. Emily nodded and took her seat, placing a stuffed-animal-shaped backpack on the chipped tile floor beneath her feet. She stared down for a while, then

30

straightened.

" Fine. Fuck you assholes. I'm Emily Zaragosza, Blood of Julian Dante, Blood of Lady Elizabeth Pillory, Blood of Marcoszius of Antioch. I'm twenty six, I was born in 1984 in Teaneck, New Jersey. I was Created by Rite of Heretic Blood on Christmas Eve, 1999."

There was silence, then laughter. I have to admit, I was a little shocked.

" So let me get this straight..." implored Khounus-Hetef.

" You were a vampire for one week?" guffawed Jennifer.

" Fuck this." Emily gathered her bags.

I straightened up. "Don't go."

"No, I'm gonna go. Clearly, I'm not old enough to have any...-"

"Are you lying, Eve?" I snapped.

"What?" Eve was taken aback, wreathed in a putrid haze.

" Are you lying about Emily? Did she or did she not spend any part of the last hundred years as a goddamned vampire?"

" Well, yes, but..."

"Great." I was fed up. I pointed to Emily. "You, sit your ass down. The rest of you, shut up. Someone say something fucking personal." I snarled.

Silence, stretched out just a bit too long. Eve broke the chill.

"Is that blood on your collar, Michael?"

I looked down, pulling out my shirt to get a better view. Sure enough, a tiny tomato-red splatter fading slowly to an ugly brown. I must not have washed this shirt since the bodega. That was... really stupid.

" Oh. Yeah, I ran into a guy with a bloody nose."

" Yeah, I bit a guy's nose off at a Circle Jerks Show in '81," offered Eve, a peculiar conversational olive branch if ever there was one.

" Holy shit, the blood. Like a fucking faucet. We were gonna do something with it for Samhain, but none of the Elders would go for drinking nosebleed."

I took the bait.

" Nosebleed, eh? I thought the savage Heretics didn't have any lines they wouldn't cross?"

" Nah, that was it. I knew a Vrykolas who'd stalk pregnant bitches for weeks, just to get at the soft stuff inside. Called it Softshell Crab. But even he wouldn't drink nosebleed."

She sneered at Emily, as if challenging the newcomer. Emily's expression didn't change.

"Jared Pelamoq, and he called it Softshell Shrimp. Get it? Because babies are small? He's a landscaper in Taos, now. I have his cell number if your like."

Eve backed off, impressed. " You ain't one of us... but whatever the fuck you are, you can stay."

As we packed up, Eve screeched.

" Jesus shit-humping Christ! What kind of asshole raises a diseased monkey of a kid who leaves a goddamned turd in his desk? I put my fucking bag in there! "

I stifled a giggle. " You put your bag in one of the desks?"

"Not fucking funny, Daghlian. Fuck Brooklyn! Fuck the outer Boroughs, fuck this school, fuck everything!"

Emily picked up the bag. "Actually, it's kind of funny."

" Bitch, I will fucking cut your...-"

" Jesus, chill out." Emily wiped the dirty brown from the small, black, shiny purse with a wadded napkin. " It's a fucking candy bar, see? Probably a fat kid."

Eve nodded slowly and took the bag, storming off in a huff. I stood before Donovan and Emily, waiting for them to gather their things before flicking out the light.

Donovan pointed. "Noticed you didn't tell her about the booger smeared on her chair."

Emily shrugged. " Comedy. Best served cold."

" That... doesn't make any..."

I switched off the dirty yellow light. We moved wordlessly though the halls, passing a sleeping security guard on the way out the front door. Donovan offered me an inscrutable look and made his way to somewhere he felt comfortable. I walked awkwardly alongside Emily until she turned to talk to me.

"You're headed to the train?"

I shrugged. "Yeah."

" Strange. Most of you older guys have a car or something. Did you not save up at all?"

" Something like that."

We walked quietly along the black and brown streets of Brooklyn.

" So, DPBR, hunh? I'll bet that's a trip."

" It's...something."

" Hundreds of years and you wind up as a social worker for misfit halloween costumes. Is that how you thought you'd finish out?"

I glowered. " I'm not 'hundreds of years' old. I'm..."

She crossed her arms and shot me a look. My shoulders fell. " I'm... one hundred and thirteen."

"Jesus christ! That's crazy. You're a hundred and thirteen. Jesus. Do you have any idea how crazy that is? When'd you change?"

I thought back.

" Umn... I guess it was nineteen twenty five. I remember a new story about the Shenandoah going down..."

" Was that a ship?"

" Dirigible."

" No fucking way! Did you ever fly in a dirigible?"

" A couple..."

" Fuck off. That's crazy as hell."

" Wait... Why?"

" Oh, you know. I was brought up by Heretics. They never got as old as the Vampires in the Society."

I stopped and adjusted my scarf.

" No, I mean.. why did you come out tonight? You were a vampire for a week. You can forget it, ignore it, like it was a bad flu. Why come commiserate with people whose whole worlds have changed?"

" What makes you think mine didn't? "

I nodded, defeated.

" Thing is, Mike- can I call you Mike?- I feel cheated. I was gypped. For one week, I was everything I had ever wanted to be. And then, before I could really even get a chance to fix anything that had been broken in my life with these new tools- poof!" She blew across her small palm, wrapped in a knit fingerless glove. " It's gone. And... you know... everyone else is still dead."

33

I put my hands in my pockets and hunched my shoulders against a bitter wind coming in from the river. She suddenly looked up at me, looking impossibly young and vulnerable in the dim orange and yellow light of the sign for the Manhattan Train. Glittering eyes of endless depth and beauty flashed from behind thick black frames and she gently touched my face as though I were terribly wounded.

" A hundred years..."

I made a face.

" Yeah... it doesn't work that way. Something we learned pretty early on is that the mind - maybe it was the blood? You processed time a certain way, refreshing around every ten years, so that the weight of it all didn't... crush you completely."

" So you forgot?"

" No. But it felt like maybe it happened to someone else. A really old guy like Khnous-Hetef or Kahfi might have forgotten more, I don't know..."

" Tell me a memory."

" Fine." I leaned against the green-painted ironwork of the subway entrance, trying to remember one that didn't require a lot of explanation.

"... Let's see..."

" Tell me something obscure, something no one else would know about."

" One of the biggest Vampiric gatherings in North American history was on April 28, 1930, in Independence, Kansas."

She raised an eyebrow.

" No bullshit. We even called a truce between the Heretics and the Society. Kahfi, Jericho Walker, T'isparigo, Jon Braxton, Bacchos Sporagmos, and Septimus Victor were all there. Vampires came from literally all over the country to a podunk little burg in the middle of Auntie Em cornfield-area Kansas... I mean, it was safer to walk the streets of any major American city that night... "

" What was it? Some sort of summit meeting?"

" Something like that. It was the first ever official night game in baseball. The Muskogee Chiefs versus the Independence Producers. I remember one guy mentioning to his boss that although the turnout

34

was good, they weren't moving a whole hell of a lot of popcorn..."

She laughed.

" Minor leagues. It was a gimmick for turnout, and the the turnout was predictably huge, because every Blooded baseball fan in the country showed up. I mean everyone. I sat between a Vrykolas from Anchorage and a couple Sangsue that had come in from Oahu. I think there was something like one vampire for every ten normal people in the crowd. We all agreed not to feed at the game, and most people didn't even feed in town at all, because we wanted them to do it it again, you know? I didn't even care about the game. I wasn't paying attention. It was so nice to sit among actual families, normal people cheering and acting so... happy. Before then the crowds were all in theaters or burlesque clubs, you know? It was so bracing..."

I paused, letting the nostalgia overtake me.

" So anyway, the night was kinda warm ...and I remember buying some roasted peanuts just so I could have them in my lap in smell them. I just kept picking one out and dropping it under the bleachers. I told the Sangsue I did it to blend in, but we all know what I was doing. Pretending."

I stared at the Empire State Building, it's top lit with orange and swathed in darkness for halloween. She looked where I was staring, then back at me.

" Michael? When was the last time you went to a baseball game?"

I looked at her blankly.

" For that matter, when was the last time you had roasted peanuts?"

I shook my head apologetically, as though I just failed a test. She pulled me towards her and kissed me ever so gently, running her hands over my face, her touch a syrupy-sweet mixture of apprehension and pity. No. I pulled her in, bit her perfect red lip and grabbed a handful of her hair. She gave in. I pulled back, shook my head.

" I... I'm..."

She put a finger to my lips.

" Ah ah. No. You say nothing, Michael Cage."

I nodded. She walked down onto the train, and I stood there a while, watching her go.

I pushed out through the stale, sweaty air of the bar, out into the cool wetness outside. A thin drizzle tapped down upon my face and I pulled my tattered coat around myself, more out of habit than any actual desire to get out of the rain. I rode the train quietly, a Gatorade bottle full of stolen whisky my only companion, and had a pretty solid buzz going by the time I got home.

I stepped up the stairs to my place, kicking the door open. Cats scattered at my approach, dashing off into the overgrown weeds in front of the boarded-up building. My apartment, such as it was, was't mine, but a place we'd broken into in when her car was impounded. I guess it was a crackhouse for a while, but we'd laid claim and no one else seemed terribly interested.

She lay, supine, across a fetid couch wearing nothing but one fishnet stocking and a stained Babydoll T with a tattered logo for Empire Erotica circa 1997. Her pink and black hair fell loose around her heavily tattooed shoulders. She played a jarringly new and shiny game console attached to a new and shiny TV. I was surprised we even still had electricity, until I saw the orange cord going out the window.

" What... Where'd you get this?" I asked.

" Stole it. Get out of my way, I'm fighting a fucking Hydra."

" No such thing as Hydras."

I slumped next to her and she sat up, not taking her eyes off the screen as she swilled a warm beer and jabbed furiously at the controls.

" How'd you do?" She asked.

" I made five hundred bucks. That's enough for next week, right?"

" Ah, fucking bug chasers for drug money. My mom'd be so proud I decided to spread for you."

" Shit, baby, if this is about pissing off your parents, shouldn't I be a black guy?"

" Fuck off. My parents met at Berkley, they'd hold my jaw open for you if you were a black guy."

I kissed her, slapping the controller from her hand. She smoothly ran a hand down my chest, into my pants, encircling the thickness in a no-nonsense way, then jabbed her thumbnail into the base of my cock. I banged her head off of the edge of the couch, and she cracked me in the temple with the beer bottle, hard enough to make me dizzy. She wiped her head with her forearm, sat back down, and un-paused the game.

" Lemme kill this guy first."

" Sure! Fine! Fucking Christ!" I rubbed my head.

" Do not fuck with me while I'm playing, Madison. I will hurt you."

" Oh, really?"

I stood up and dug myself out of my pants. In response, she broke the bottle, still watching the screen, and pointed the ragged glass at my stiffening genitals. I dipped myself gently back into my pants and headed toward the room that was once the kitchen, now a grey series of counters and a mouldering hole where a sink used to be. " Fine. What do we have to eat in here?"

" Gin."

" That'll do."

I pulled the bottle from the counter and took a bracing chug, savoring the burn as it went down and returned to my place next to her.

" So I fucked a skinhead to keep us in crystal another week. What did you do tonight?"

" I found him. He wants me so bad his fucking balls hurt."

There are so few occasions that one does a spit-take out of genuine surprise and not just for emphasis. I

37

wasn't sure if this was one of those times, but I wasn't about to waste good alcohol on it. Instead, I made a wet noise and doubled over, forcing it down despite its unexpected field trip to my sinuses and tear ducts. Wiping my nose on my sleeve, I turned to her. Reached for her, reconsidered, and got up behind her and started gently rubbing her neck and shoulders, as if to imply that I meant no interference in the game. She paused and looked back at me.

"Holy shit. This means a lot to you." She grinned.

" You will never know." I kissed her head, trying as hard as I could to impart nothing but warmth and admiration.

" He's not much, you know. Cute, I guess. Your age, maybe a little heavier."

The revelation boggled me. I hadn't really seen him up close. I hardened a bit.

" Michael Cage got fat!?"

" I dunno. More like soft. You're definitely in better shape than him."

I looked down at myself. "I have AIDS and I'm addicted to Crystal Meth. That... That can't be right."

"He's been like a suburban social worker guy for ten years, you know- eating real food. What do you expect? Sometimes I think you haven't eaten anything but Vicodin since you started breathing."

I thought about that. Couldn't prove her wrong.

"So yeah, I guess he's heavier. And, you know, older. Like you."

"Fuck yourself."

"You first, New Deal."

I sighed, enjoying her girly squeal as the Hydra collapsed to the ground, all heads neatly defeated.

"So now what happens?"

"Stay with him. I promised to deliver him and that's exactly what we'll do."

* * * *

" They ran back into town and hid in the church
They explained their situation and they feared for the worst
The priest told the brothers that she could not be killed
She flew out of the stone cold ground and
She'll find you and she'll kill you
She'll find you and she'll kill you
She'll find you and she'll kill you"
Chad VanGaalen, "Molten Light"

Michael awoke, fetal, suffused with stabbing into every joint of his body. Suit stuck to his skin. A basement? Cold air and wet concrete, only comfort a tattered grey-and blue woolen comforter. Glass in his eyes and hands. He tried to get up, slipped in something warm and wet. Haze; pain, wanted to cry. Sadness, hopelessness like a fever, like a virus in his skull, hammering at his armpits and his knees and groin and then vomit.

"Huuaaaghh! Guh-Aigh!" He tried to scream again but instead heaved up a great cold yellow mess, curdled and foaming and half-solid like old egg whites. The fluid was thick and fibrous and refused to leave his mouth or his tongue; he inhaled and accidentally sucked it back in, salty and vile. It made him puke again, and this time it all came free, along with something rubbery, grey and solid. Intricately veined. Alive. Part of him. He screamed again, and the scream brought more pain, along with a tearing sound and a cold wet run along his thigh. He tried to stop it but it flowed from his ass, nostrils, and flaccid prick like warm milk. The sickness was everywhere.

"WhatisthisWHATISTHIS?"

He collapsed into a pool of his own making, trying to keep it together.

"Whuh? Where? Why?"

Lying in a pool of coagulating fluid, crying tears of salty pus, he pulled the slime-wetted blanket around himself and begged for sleep that would not come. He cried. So hungry. And she came to him and fed him and made him sleep, and he was too happy, too comforted to ask anyone why.

He awoke, erect, hazy, confused. So hungry. Tried to open his eyes; couldn't. Tried to move his hand, couldn't. Wrenched it out of grainy scab, picked half-inch of crust from one eye. Noted with alarm the blood in it. Noted was still in basement. Slimy mess now hard and gritty; stink curling like poison gas. He sat up, hearing the crunch as he put his hand down one the woolen blanket now scabbed over unto a crumpled horseshoe shape. The stink was overwhelming and yet felt like it was happening to someone else entirely. Michael stood up and looked for a window, but there was none. The room was four walls of concrete and a filthy floor covered with a drain.

" Hello? Hello?"

So hungry.

Echo. Voice thin and scratchy from unconscious screaming. How long had it been? He was naked now, clothes kicked into a rumpled corner, also solid with crust of dried humours. He stood. Put a hand on the wall. Cold, definitely underground. Dark. Moved his hand up along the concrete. Unseen insects skittered away from his fingertips. Felt around. Felt wood on wall overhead. Felt glass. A window? A basement window, high up? Michael took a step back, looked. The glass was obscured by something, blacked over. He tapped it. It was covered in a layer of something thin- paint? Had the window been painted over? He scratched at the paint...

Pain!

He yanked his hand back, smelling burnt flesh. Fear again went from universal to focused. A sliver of light lanced through the jagged scratch he'd made in the window's paint. Shaking off the confusion, he moved to peer through the-

Pain!

Collapsed, screaming, screaming, screaming. The burn was unholy, it pierced him, excised him, judged him like an authority. He tried to stop screaming and couldn't, like a child with his first burn. Both hands covered his eye and he swore he smelled smoke rising from the socket. In his writhing, his elbow crossed the light, renewing the almighty pain. More screaming, cursing.

40

He scuttled to the furthest corner away from the piercing light, a single shaft in which dust floated and danced innocently, and he still felt it, still hated it, like the desert sun on the back of a dying man. It was too bright, too hot, too deadly. He gathered the repugnant wool blanket and mashed it into the windowpane, blotting out the hateful light.

He tried to make sense of it. tried to think clearly, but the confusion and total alienation of the situation was overwhelming. He sobbed, tried to remember, but everything before this room was a haze. He remembered Laura. She smiled and said yes, didn't she? That was nice. Hold on to that. Hold onto that. You need to sleep now. Sleep.

* * * *

I woke up and sat upright, looked over at where Laura slept. Wandered into the bathroom and blinked at my reflection- black hair, no longer as thick as it once was. Eyes puffy. Skin, darker. Thickening midsection. Contact lens case on the soap dish. Bum wrist that ached when it rained. Splashing water on my face, I slicked my now reasonably-cropped hair flat against my head, noticing imperceptible lines around my eyes and I know how Vernon felt.

I have every reason to be ashamed of this, given what I once was.
Fire away.
No. Don't listen. Do something else. Television. Play with the dog. Try a video game, any form of distraction...

In my tattered shorts, I relaxed in front of the television. Switching it on, I immediately dropped the volume so as not to wake the wife, noting with some alarm the images of violence in Eastern Europe.

"Militants continue to clash on the Moldovian Border of Romania-"

No. Something easier. Colored lights flashed over me as I jumped from the news to an informercial to cartoons to sports to... wait. Back.

On ESPN, a sleek black set framed two men sitting comfortably engaging in an easy conversation. The man on the left had short red hair, a loose tie and a quizzical expression. The man on the right was easily two heads taller, dark skin, stretched earlobes and ancient ritual scarring on his face. He was a tower of coiled muscle, and even

41

relaxing in this chair he looked ready to burst into a thousand-mile-per-hour sprint.

Na'qi Kahfi.

"- and even further in the quarterfinals, right?"

"That's right, Vince. I think these guys look tight for the new season, and they should take it all they way."

"So, is that your prediction, Kahfi?"

Kahfi nodded. He was born for this, a true success story. He grew up breaking records and would continue to do so for quite a while. Most of the elders had the most trouble adjusting, but he was a weird case for an elder even at the time. There's a correlation between Recidivism and age- the older we are, the harder it was for us to adjust. Fortunately the majority of us hovered around a century- the first hundred years were always the deadliest- and by then the Purge had taken its toll. For Kahfi, a thousand years as a six-year old was more than enough.

Kahfi was almost a millennia old, created by some turn of events he didn't like to talk about in ancient Africa. He was born to a Maasai-like tribe that almost certainly no longer exists. He had spent nine centuries trapped in the body of a hyperactive child, dreaming of what it would be to to run with the legs of a man, to look down at people when he spoke to them, and the Redemption allowed him to finally realize that dream.

In the past ten years, he had broken records left and right. He had authored two books on African history, taught a course in ancient tribal dance at NYU, won four gold medals at the Olympics, and on top of it all he could bench me and my dog. Kids had "Percolator" T-shirts that were a play on the "Mr. Kahfi" name. He was perhaps second only to Jericho Walker, a true post-blooded success story.

I looked at his number on my phone, stretched. Maybe I'd call him tomorrow.

Then again, maybe not.

NEXT THURSDAY

"Entering the Milosevic vault and driving a hawthorn stake through the grave was my duty carried out in the name of the Pozarevac Resistance. I wanted to do it painlessly, without conflict with the people who would be at the grave on the day of the anniversary. After I drove the stake through the grave I presented myself at the police station and made a statement to the chief."

The late dictator's daughter-in-law, Milica Galici, has lodged a complaint over the 'violation of Milosevic's grave.' The complaint would be sent to the state prosecutor's office.

In spite of protests by Serbian nationalists, young Miroslav has achieved his aim: Milosevic is no longer an Undead 'vrykolas' able to haunt his home town.

Thanks to the hawthorn stake, Pozarevac is a safer place today. But this cannot be said about Serbia as a whole, which is still being haunted by Milosevic's nationalist spirit.

- Herald Scotland "Vampire slayer impales Milosevic to stop Return", 10 Mar 2007

I awoke, bleary, to loud barking and Laura gently rubbing my chest.
" Hyunh... ? Wha?"
" Honey? Two things. One: Where's the car?"
I rubbed my eyes. "Honey? What time did you get in last night?" Downstairs Boochie barked bloody murder at something in the front room. I looked out the window but there was no one walking past to elicit such a reaction.

She smiled. "Late, like I said. Where'd you park the car?"
I stretched. "Remember how that cabbie sideswiped me? Bent the axle. Gonna be there a few more days."

She nodded, her unusual morning cheer no more diminished for the news. This obviously struck me as odd. Shaking off the morning chill I tried to get back into my proper vision, rubbing my eyes furiously against the blur and floating spots.

" Uh. What's the second thing?"

" The second thing is that I *love* it. I love it! And on a school day! Sometimes, I just... I love you. You can still do some awesome things."

She kissed me softly, but hard enough to project her excitement. I tried to pull back, self-conscious of my morning breath, but she wasn't having it.

" Go in late today?"

" I... I..." I looked at her face and couldn't finish. I smiled and nodded. She sat upright and dashed back out of the room. I called after her.

" Honey? Honey? Wait... What? You love what?"

I sat up, and Boochie tore in and took the opportunity to leap up onto the bed. He parked at me pointedly, making it very clear that there was a situation that required my attention and WHY WASN'T I DOING SOMETHING ABOUT THIS?

Scratching my belly while trying clear something that had insistently lodged itself into one of my sinuses in the dead of night, I followed my wife downstairs. The dog, still barking madly, spun circles around my legs, then darted into the front room. I stopped and stared.

" It's totally insane! I love it!"

A freshly painted statue of an angel- clearly several hundred pounds of stone- dominated the room. She held her hands aloft in supplication, her eyes obscured by an intricate hood. It had to be seven feet tall if it was an inch. I boggled at it.

" I ... uh..."

" It's completely crazy. Where'd you find it? It looks like it came from some sort of medieval graveyard."

I approached the thing, fascinated. She looked at me, her smile dropping a bit.

" Michael? Where'd you find it?"

I shook my head.

" I... I... Did someone else get you this? Your gallery guy?"

She looked hurt, then, confused.

" No. Julian wouldn't... this is really not his style. He'd have gone for something more abstract, maybe... so you didn't...?"

I tried to convince myself that I hadn't just asked to prevent any future confusion. Fuck it. She was happy. With *me*. I looked down, then back at her, doing my best "ya got me" smile.

" I got it in Rome, back in '63. I bought it but never got around to bringing it back here. Forgot I owned it until I got the storage bill, so I figured, what the hell, right? So you like it?"

For a second I think she could tell I was lying, but then made a conscious decision not to care. She threw her arms around me.

" See? Somewhere in there, you're still a madman. That's swell."

" That's *awesome*, baby." I corrected. "Awesome. People say "awesome" now."

" You're fresh."

" That's still kinda atavistic."

" Nuh-uh," She pouted. "I'm bringing it back. Want coffee?" She moved into the kitchen, still considering it.

" Does anyone say def any more?"

" No one with any melanin."

" What about Def Jam? Like Def Jam records?"

" That was named, like, 30 years ago."

She paused over the counter.

" No shit?"

" No shit."

She puzzled around the kitchen, fidgeting with a fridge magnet. Tried it out: " This soup is a real Def Jam."

I put my hands on her shoulders. " Honey... please. Stop."

" Have you tried the salmon? 'Cuz 's stoopid fresh."

" Leaving..." I announced, heading back into the living room with my coffee. She darted in after I took a long, slow sip.

" Who do you think made it?"

I shrugged. Something about the lines seemed familiar, yet wrong. I poked at it.

" What'd the packing slip say?"

46

She shrugged. "I dunno. I got down here and found it like this."
I sank a bit.

" No one called or anything? It just showed up here?"

" Nope. Just- poof, here it is."

That didn't sound at all good. I tried to backpedal.

" Laura? I had a lot of... enemies in the sixties. Mind if I... double check this thing, make sure it's safe?"

She gave me a look to ask if I was kidding. I shook my head. She nodded and headed upstairs.

" I need to get to the city before noon to set up the framing. Can we get dinner out there, tonight? Maybe I can meet you at your office?"

Sh came down, dressed, bright red back slung over one shoulder. She looked at me, then the statue, kissed my cheek, then stopped for a quick breath to admire the statue again. She patted my hair, mouthed the words, "*I love it!*", and bounced out the door.

I relaxed. I figured it wasn't safe to leave it with her, for some reason. I poked around the statue again. If it was a bomb or something, it was long dead- the statue was clearly a few dozen years old at least, judging by the wear, I'd guess considerably older. Fuck it. It looked good there and it made Laura happy. Let it be for now.

* * * *

" Hey, Mike! Hows' it goin,' man?"

I illegally shouldered my phone while shooting up Sixth Avenue, wary of any bored-looking cops.

" Good, good. Say, you in town? I need help with a case." I asked.

" I'm at a publisher right now but I got the afternoon free." Kahfi said.

" Publisher?"

" Working on my memoirs."

" Fucking hell, man. You're physically what- eighteen?"

" I'm older than your whole country, bitch."

" You're older than dirt. You up in midtown?"

" Yeah, man. Harper-Collins."

" Sure. I saw you on ESPN Last Night, you're looking well." I offered.

" I got my ears pierced."

" You... always had..."

" No, I got new ones. In the top."

" I missed that. Say, you wanna get together? Get some lunch?"

" Sure, man. You free next week?"

I turned onto Fourteenth, scanning in futility for a parking space anywhere near Union Square.

" Next week. I think I can do that. I'm driving, can you email me? Let's hook it up."

" Where do you wanna go?"

My phone beeped. Incoming. I looked at it, and a number I didn't recognize glowed back at me.

" I dunno. I got an incoming call, but I'll hook up with you over email, OK?"

" You bet. Lates!"

I pulled into a garage and clicked over the call.

" This is Daghlian."

" Michael Daghlian? Dr. Kreitzer. We spoke last week?"

" Oh? Oh! Oh, yeah, hey!" I mumbled as I pulled into the garage next to a brightly colored stock van wrapped in decals for a radio station. I hopped out of the car and handed the tall man in the polo shirt walking toward me my keys, noting that it was all reflex and hoping he was actually, in fact, the parking attendant and not some random kid. He nodded at me.

" How long?"

I covered the phone with my palm.

" An hour?"

He handed me a ticket stub.

" Hey, so I wanted to know if you wanted to get that beer this weekend?" asked Kreitzer.

" Uh... sure. Sure!"

" Great. I got a shift free and my kid's staying with her mom this week. You know Fat Black Pussycat near 6th?"

" Yeah."

I walked through Union Square park toward Sixteenth, noticing

48

the warmth in the air despite how late in the month it had gotten. The benches were crowded with the couples and the elderly, and dogs filled the dog run. I felt like it should have been colder.

" I'll be there at seven Saturday. There's this waitress there who doesn't know I'm a doctor and I've been hitting on her for two weeks."

" I... I don't get it...."

" You get tired of just getting laid because of your job, you know?"

" I'm a glorified social worker, Doc."

" Yeah, but you used to be a vampire. You know what I'm talking about."

I stopped. He was right.

" Touché, doc."

" See you there."

I hung up and headed up to see my 2:00.

I sat in a well-appointed living room in a Union Square apartment that had been rent-controlled since the seventies. The couch was supposed one on which Allen Ginsberg traded dirty jokes with Lenny Bruce, and the table was rumored to have been one where Lou Reed did lines with Malcolm McLaren after a legendary rooftop shindig that no one ever knew about. There was a cracked hardhat stolen from the riots of the same name, and a flyer for an underground punk show Sid Vicious was supposed to appear at but wound up indisposed.

I stared at Nigel Huxley's Basquiat . He stood in the kitchen mixing "tea" for us, which was less suspect this time.

" I heard about Vernon." He said in his manicured accent, carrying a silver tray into the room. Pouring for me, he shook his head sadly.

" Poor Vernon. Too beautiful for dignity."

I raised an eyebrow. He held his cup aloft.

" To immortality, Michael."

I nodded and drank. It was bitter and made my tongue itch.

" Whu... what's in this, Nigel? I thought we agreed no more hallucinogens."

" We did. It's an extinct Moroccan herb called *Fenndeng*. You know how Chinese people insist on grinding up all manner of God's creatures in an attempt to cure impotence? The Moors sold them this and they've been trying to replicate it ever since."

I immediately felt a pleasant but urgent rush.

" Wh... why would you give me this?"

" Oh, relax, Michael. I'm not going to try and fuck you. It's *funny*. Erections are *funny*. Our new bodies are tragic, hilarious."

I hunched forward, scratching absentmindedly at my scalp.

" Not exactly new bodies... it's just what we started with."

" Lighten up! There must be something we get out of this."

" We get a lot out of it, Nigel. Sunlight? Food? Life without murder?"

He sighed at me.

" There's no such thing as life without murder, Michael. I know your secret, and I can feel it draining into regret. Look at your face, man. You look so tired, so ...beaten. "

I shook my head.

"How is Laura?" He pressed.

I backed off. " Nigel, I'm fine. She's fine."

" Oh, fine. Fine never is."

" We're not here to talk about me, Nigel."

" And yet, here we are..."

I leaned forward more, feeling the swelling bloom. I hunkered left in an attempt to push it in a comfortable direction. He smiled at his little joke, and I decided against bringing up the fact that he hadn't seemed to have dosed himself. That would only push the conversation further into territory I didn't want it to go into.

" OK, Nigel. Any urges, cravings, or desire for blood in the past month?"

" Every walking moment of every day, just like you."

I raised my eyebrows at him.

" You really want me to say that?"

He sighed. " ... No."

I marked it down.

" How do you sleep?"

" Heroin."

" Careful, that stuff'll kill you, now."

" If only."

I shook my head. He got up and crossed to the painting, admiring it. " And you keep your bloody judgements to myself. You're here to see if I'm a fucking vampire, not a drug addict. I am a drug addict. I'm still *something*, Michael. What are you?"

I ignored the question. " I'm a guy doing my job, Nigel. So, have you experienced any funny smells, strange sounds, or visual hallucinations?"

He raised an eyebrow at me. I nodded apologetically.

" Have you attended any Coven or Bloodline meetings, or have you found yourself following individuals of a savory nature?"

Nigel turned back to me from the painting.

" What the fuck does that mean, "Individual of a savory nature? "

" I dunno. Tasty people."

" ...No." He emphasized his answer so as to assure me that the very act of answering the question degraded him.

" Are we done, Michael? Do you have any more questions?"

" Just one."

He breathed deep, waving me to go on.

" How long until this goes down again? "

Dinner was awkward.

* * *

"Michael Cage. The Council recognizes Michael Cage, Blood of Leucretia Dominique,

Blood of The Carpathian. " Vernon Grange sniffed. He stood to the left of the Prefect of Philadelphia as a council of Vampires regarded the two newcomers before them, dressed like rock stars and glowering like soldiers.

It was 1975, and Michael Cage was seventy-eight years old. He wore a knee-length dark brown leather coat, jeans, and a wide-collar shirt, open to reveal a gold cross on his chest, which he wore exclusively because he appreciated the irony. His hair was dark and he wore it long; his eyes were darker and he hid them behind tinted glasses, as most of his kind did. He looked the exact age he'd been when he'd turned, twenty-eight. It was a good age for it. Too young-looking, the elders didn't take you seriously. Too old, you appeared feeble. Leucretia had had plans for him, and she was old enough that patience was something she measured in decades.

Michael looked to his companion. Ben Dreyfuss shifted uneasily, sniffing the air. He stood apart. The others in the room tolerated Cage, but there was a inexplicable primal terror that gripped them at Dreyfuss' presence. He stood six and half feet tall, with long shaggy blonde hair and the easy grey eyes of a much older man. Dreyfuss looked to be in his early twenties. He wore dirty jeans, a black leather cowboy hat, motorcycle boots and a white T-shirt emblazoned with a humanoid figure within a circle with a line through it.

No humans.

Dreyfuss shrugged at Michael, who waved him down with his hand. "I've got this."

He stepped forward.

"Kneel before the Prefect, Cage."

Michael wanted to sigh but he knew better. He took a knee. Walker Jericho spun in his chair and looked down at him.

"Rise, Cage," he said with a deep baritone. "Tell us what brings you here."

Jericho had been born in Philadelphia since the Revolutionary War and took pride in the fact that while he may have grown up a slave, this city, at least, had become his in return. Vernon "Croglin" Grange, his chief Lictor and Majordomo, had been a farmer who had actually been sent to kill him by Hessian assassins. Vernon had eventually double-crossed his former masters, a ballsy move that led to his cushy position here.

They sat in a secret rotunda about two hundred feet under Independence Hall, a hastily-chiseled edifice once used for smuggling weapons, but now a meeting hall for the city's vampires, or the

"Blooded", as they referred to themselves. The Prefect of Philadelphia sat on a raised bench above his subjects, not unlike a courtroom. It was but one of dozens of secret chambers of its kind- nearly every major city on the globe had one. Philadelphia's Rotunda reflected the city's former glory. While some parts of the room were clearly just hewn bedrock, the great vaulted ceiling was painted in a faded but ostentatious pattern of stars and stripes and dated 1777. Cage looked up at it and shuffled nervously, realizing that the symbol that hovered above them all meant nothing to any of them, and was simply allowed to remain there as a memento of the rotunda's history, nothing more. He inhaled deeply and stood, staring Jericho in the eye.

"Prefect, I came all the way from Chicago with a formal request. My companion and I have painstakingly drafted a plan of attack by which we believe we can retake New York City. We would like to...-"

Jericho cracked a wry grin, his expression a curious mix of contempt and pity.

"I appreciate what you're trying to do. But I can't in good conscience let you charge to your death, Cage. So many...- "

"Dozens have tried to take the city back from Breughel, and all have failed, I know. I feel that I have a very different idea."

"They all said that. Everett Granger thought he could use zeppelins to do it in the 20's. Timothy Ellefson attempted to walk an army of invaders across the floor of the Hudson. The Holland Tunnel itself was a thinly-disguised attempt by Lydia Frances Hood. It's a waste of time." Jericho smiled. " Your dedication to The Society is noted, and appreciated, Cage. Wolfgang Breughel and his Heretical Archdiocese have held the city for nearly a century now. You would die needlessly, and I just can't spare the resources you would need for an assault."

" I don't need any resources. Humor me, Prefect. Just hear me out."

The Prefect cocked and eyebrow and, for the first time, looked directly at Cage.

" No resources?"

"No, your Highness. I would simply require the ability to pass through your city unhindered to do what I need to do. I'll be buying weapons, talismans, moving personnel. Of course, there is the matter of New York needing a prefect once we've re-taken it."

"You... don't want to take the title?"

"Not really. I wish to live there, not to rule it, your Highness."

"Nice gambit. Alright, Cage, you've got my attention. How do you and your breathing friend plan to take New York by yourselves?"

"Oh, ya caught that, didja?" Ben smiled. "Ben Dreyfuss, yer Highness. It's an honor."

"Right."

The prefect never looked at Ben, keeping his eyes locked on Cage.

"He spoke out of turn. He's not even supposed to be here, I hope you've got him on a short..-"

"I'm gonna have to cut you off right there before you make a very big mistake, Prefect."

Jericho glared at him. Michael stepped forward to diffuse the situation. He looked to Ben.

"It's time, Ben. Show them. Show them why you're here."

Ben smiled, nodded and peeled his shirt off over his head.

" Mister Cage..."

Ben's muscles rippled, his nails blackened, and there was a sickening sound- the stretching of skin and the popping and snapping of bone. A grunt escaped his lips lowering steadily in pitch until it became a growl.

"No.... NO!" Croglin leapt over the bench and cringed behind it. The Prefect stared, his jaw slack, as his Lictors uselessly moved to shield his body. The council got to their feet, some cried out, others made for the door. Michael waved his arms.

"There's no danger! Everyone stay calm!"

Walker Jericho stared in rapt terror at the eight-foot wall of white fur and muscle that stood where the wiry boy had been. It was hunched like an ape, with hooked, wicked claws, a shaggy tail, and large, canine head. The creature grinned impishly at the panic it was causing, tongue lolling between jagged teeth.

"Lycanthrope." whispered the Prefect.

A shot rang out- one of the Prefect's Lictors held a handgun out in his trembling hand. The bullet seemed to no more than get the creature's attention and it swiveled its massive head at him. Michael burst forward and slapped the gun down.

"No! No!"

"At ease, Lictor." Jericho rose to his feet, staring at the werewolf in the center of the room. "Everyone silent! Calm down!" He turned to Michael.

"How did you do this, Cage? Lycanthropes can't be dominated or controlled."

"Contrary t' pop'lar opinion, can... be reason'd with." barked the monster.

Walker's eyes went wide.

" Ben Dreyfuss is a pack alpha. They're willing to help me. We can do this, your Highness. We just need your support."

"You... make for a very convincing case, Mr. Cage."

ABSOLUTION

NEXT FRIDAY

"Surprise! you're dead!
Ha ha! open your eyes
See the world as it used to be when you used to be in it
When you were alive and when you were in love
And when I took it from you! "
  - Faith No More, "Surprise, You're dead!"

I stared at my reflection, long and hard.
You asked for this.
You fought for this.
You want this.
You *deserve* this, for what you've done.
I put on my shirt and grabbed my coat.

As I hung up my coat at the office, Tricia rushed up to me. She looked anxious, and immediately started absentmindedly fidgeting with my tie.

"Uh... Braxton's here, and he's pissed about something. Wants to see you."

" Great." I withdrew my tie from her tightening grip. " Did he say what about?"

She shook her head.

" No, but he had that sword again, Mr. Daghlian. That's never a good sign."

"No. No, I guess it's not."

I walked into Braxton's office and noticed that the polished wood plaque on the wall which held up his old longsword was empty. So was his chair. I moved into the room.

" Jon?"

" Not now! I'm shitting, Daghlian, do you realize how fucking sacred this is? I waited half a millennia for movements such as these and should you interrupt this symphony any further I swear I shall twist your head off your neck and dance in the blood fountain."

I nodded and took a seat, looking around the well-appointed room. Well-appointed for civil service, anyway. Waited maybe twenty minutes, trying not to hear the satisfied grunts following every weighty splash. Finally he came out, waving the sword.

" Daghlian. Have a seat. Shut the door."

I noticed I was already sitting and the door was well closed. He crossed to his desk and slid back into his chair and breathed in deeply.

" Fucking Washington." He exhaled.

" Did you get anywhere with the Education act?"

He shook his head. I decided to change the topic.

" I got the new reports from Bianchi's department about..."

" Don't worry about Bianchi. We've other things to discuss. Specifically, a few days ago, police found an armed man with a record of prior convictions about two blocks from here with a fucking razor blade rammed into his fucking sinuses. According to the officer's report, it was -" He pulled a sheet of paper from his desk and read from it. "- the fucking bloodiest fucking thing he'd ever fucking seen."

His eyes drifted back up to me from the page.

" Thoughts?"

I gave him a contemplative look. He continued.

" A Korean woman at a nearby deli claimed he tried to rob the place before he was viciously attacked by a short man in a light shirt and tie, with dark eyes and black hair. She said he "seemed to enjoy seeing the gunman experience pain. "

Guilty. Shit. I gave him nothing.

" You know how this looks?"

I breathed slowly, nodding at him as if we were both judging someone else.

" Now, the investigation's been shelved because someone owes me a big favor, Mr. Daghlian."

" I didn't...-"

He pointed the broadsword directly at me. I noted with some alarm this sight, in a different context, was the very last thing that several hundred Moors had ever seen. He turned the blade, as if to riposte whatever I was about to say.

" Ah-ah, Daghlian. Say nothing. Not a word. I don't want to know your side because you don't have a side. This thing happened and you may well have been fucking your secretary at the time. Got it? Am I crystal fucking clear?"

I nodded again, silently.

" The gentleman in question was wanted on two counts of rape and aggravated assault and another account of selling schedule 2 narcotics in a school zone. So, to use our old parlance, this gentleman was *exquisite* prey- no one would have missed him, and most people involved feel he deserved what happened to him. Which would be a happy ending, were it the fucking *point*. But the fucking *point*, as gentlemen like *us* know, is that were any member of our department to have had *anything* to do with this would indicate the presence of an active and precise hunting instinct."

He rapped the sword on his desk for effect.

" And we don't need that, because we eat fucking sandwiches here. Are we clear? Were Jericho or the media or God-for-fucking-bid Anthony Bianchi to come through here at lunchtime and find a single one of us with anything but a sandwich, you see how badly this could spiral out of our fucking control? Yes. Yes, of course you do."

He placed the broadsword down, gently, across his blotter.

" I've worked hard for this department. So have you. So have Lofgren, Peters and Dakini. And all of us have a very different sense of loyalty to an idea, than, say, the people at the technical school one floor down. "

He softened.

" I want to fuck Anthony Bianchi's daughter while he and his wife are tied to the stove. And she's fourteen, man. Fourteen. I want to *make* her in front of his face, Daghlian. Very, very badly. You know what I did this morning? I sent his department a fruit basket. Because that's how we make our fucking points now. Do you understand?"

He pulled a white cloth from the jacket of his suit and ran it along the blade, as if cleaning off imaginary blood.

" Go home, Michael Daghlian. Go see your wife for a while, maybe take a vacation. We'll call you when this is fixed and you can come back in, all right? But for now, you're better off..."

He breathed on the silvery metal, and buffed it out.

"You're better off somewhere else."

I slunk back down the hall to my office, blank-faced, past Tricia, who tried to tell me something I didn't hear, until I walked into my office. Emily looked over at me as though I had just arrived late to a meeting, and sound flooded back into my world, just in time to hear the last of what she'd tried to tell me in the hall.

" -...And she said she had a meeting with you at lunch."

I turned to the door.

" Well, here she is. Thanks, Trish. Anything else?"

She shook her head. I nodded and closed the door. Turned back to Emily. She wore a small T-shirt, some sort of pleather miniskirt, and huge, knee-high boots that didn't actually match. She smiled at me.

" Let's get Korean! It wasn't too hard to find you from the...-"

I lunged across the room to her, gathered her up in my arms, kissed her deeply enough to make it clear I wasn't asking. She answered perfectly, grabbing a big angry handful of my hair and pulling me in. I reached in and hooked a thumb under the crotch of her panties, pulling them off like a gum wrapper as she undid my tie, ripped open my shirt, and pulled my belt away. I pulled her shirt up over her head, grabbing a handful of her right breast and burying myself in the soft, tattooed skin. A series of stars along her collarbone traced my my way down, and I pulled her breast free, taking her nipple into my mouth without looking, feeling a metal barbell clicking against my teeth. Well how about that.

She grabbed my cock expertly, that reverse samurai-sword grip perfected only by other men, porn stars, and only the most insane and enthusiastic women. Stroking urgently, she pulled me close and pressed my swollen head against her freshly-shaved cunt. I bit down and tugged on her nipple as I pushed in, easily, like she was expecting this. She kissed me again and braced herself with her free hand as I fucked her on the desk.

" Jesus Christ. Where's this coming from?" she panted.

" Do you actually care?"

She shook her head no. I kissed her neck. She had a point. I knew this would happen. Who was I angry with? Laura? Valentine? Jon? No. Bianchi? No. I didn't like him, but it wasn't this kind of emotion. The desk rocked with every thump, and she let another gasp escape her lips. I moved back to her neck, tracing the line of her pulse, where just under the surface, she waited for me.

" Do it." She whispered.

No. A fresh surge of hatefuck escaped my spine. I grabbed her waist and one of those cute little pigtails and lifted her, spun her, and she landed flat with a fleshy thud, her skirt now hiked up around her belly. I could see her elaborate back tattoo of the painting on the ceiling of the Sistine Chapel, and a baroque banner at the small of her back below read: " *A place beyond shame is where we belong.*"

The languid curves of her ass and thighs bent purposefully over the edge of the desk. Her sex peeked out like an invitation. I grabbed a handful of one cheek, guiding myself in with the other. She pushed back against me and swiped what few items were left on the desk to the floor. I gathered her skirt up like a bridle against her tummy, slamming slow and hard to really get my point across. The door opened.

" Mr. Daghlian, I need you to tell me where to fi- Oh my god!"

I looked over at Tricia, eyebrows raised, as if she'd somehow made this bed. She stood in shock, holding the file to her chest. And then Emily said something that made me, just in that one moment, love her.

" Hey. New chick. Get in or get out."

Tricia got out. I bent way over Emily, trying my damnedest to really feel her insides against my cock. I slipped a finger in her mouth. She bit down hard and pushed back harder. I pulled her up to a standing position, still sliding in and out of her. Moved next to her head.

" You *need* it, don't you? You won't come unless..."

She nodded. I wrenched her arm back as if to get her to say uncle, grabbed the picture of Laura off the desk, smashed it, and ran a shard of glass along the inside of her wrist. The cut bloomed red and she locked down around me, thrashing. I held the glass to her arm, noting a familiar crisscross of scars along her inner forearm, now obscuring a tattoo from her youth into a smudge. She cried out and thrashed, pulled her arm free, and braced herself against the desk, shuddering and flushed. Finally, she turned to me, a crazy half-grin on her face, and pushed me back into my chair. Licking the inside of her wrist, she dropped to her knees before me.

" I'm getting *something* out of you."

I nodded. She worked hard, both hands, the kind of blowjob that is not fucking around with anything but results. I grabbed the chair and held on, felt it well within me, and let it rush. My head swam with the force of it, draining from my balls, my shoulders, my thighs and my teeth. She choked but kept going, expertly finishing off spurt after spurt, and when I finally relaxed, she drew the last drops out of me like I was the fountain of youth.

I lay slack in the chair, shirt ruined, office ruined, pants around my ankles, taking in the absurdity of what had just transpired.

" Holy shit. What the fuck was that?" I asked. She curled into me, laying her weight on my chest. I brushed some hair out of her eyes.

" I don't fucking know. Clearly I came here on the right Tuesday. This what you normally fucking do for lunch around here?"

" I normally do tuna salad."

" That must be some deeply satisfied and well-fucked tuna salad. Jesus Christ. I thought you'd be... less... less *that*."

That sounded odd.

" You thought? You knew I'd do that?"

" I had planned for it. I figured I'd be taking the lead, but uh... no. That's... that's not what happened. Christ." She reached between her legs, as if to make sure everything was still in order down there.

" So... what do you want to do for lunch, Michael?"

I kissed her again, almost like a greeting.

" I want to do some very hard drugs and then get in a fight."

She got to her feet and nodded at me as though this was the most normal thing in the world.

* * * *

Michael Cage leaned against the table and looked at his cards, ignoring his line of sight but focusing on the figures in his peripheral vision. The room whirled and clanged and blinked but he tuned it out. The comforting weight of a pistol rested against his ribs, tucked neatly into his jacket. He had decided he liked Las Vegas. It was warm, and so was he. He could wear sunglasses or his hat down low and no one really bugged him about it. Everyone had their own agenda here and that suited him just fine. And best of all, it was open all night.

He was in the "New Frontier Hotel and Casino", which the brightly smiling lady he'd rented his room from last night explained was very recently called the "Last Frontier Hotel and Casino," but the name had been changed to reflect a more modern outlook! It was all so terribly exciting. He hadn't stayed long, just long enough to make sure all the knots were tight. After waking up at El Rancho, he came to his room here, opened the window and kicked the rope out, came down here, and started playing. Tonight was the last night of his stay, and he had been told to wait at this table for a man in a blue suit.

" Sir? Hit or stay?"

He looked at his cards. A two and a six.

" Ugh... Hit."

The dealer dropped him an eight. He shrugged his approval and scanned the room again. A thin, dark-haired man in a dark blue suit walked toward him through the crowd. He smiled.

" Actually, can you cash me out?" The dealer, a pinch-faced man with carefully groomed sideburns, nodded, waving the pit boss over. They pushed a pile of bills across the table to him.

Michael stood and faced the blue-suited man, noticing that his hair was long and bunched up under his hat to give him a more legitimate look. That wasn't normal.

" Michael Cage. I spoke with your employer on the phone?"

" You did. I'm Valery Meyer." The man smiled. " I'm afraid we don't have much time. Follow me, please?"

Michael obliged him. They headed through the casino to the elevator bank. Michael dodged a Cigarette Girl and deftly removed a martini from her tray, dropping a dollar. She winked at him. He winked back.

" You smooth fucker." Meyer smirked through a rough haze of

stubble. "Ladies treating you well out here?"

"Everything's treating me well out here."

"Where you from?"

"Atlantic City. You?"

Valery smiled. "Local boy. Been here all my life." The elevator dinged open and the two men stepped in. The elevator operator took one look at Meyer and stepped out, nodding to him like a soldier. The doors closed.

"Really? A local?" Michael mused.

"Yep."

"With a name like Valery?"

Meyer grinned, caught. "My name's Steve. But I tell the broads I'm from Paris. Trick is to come up with a kinda pussy name so it's believable."

"And that works?"

"I'm still usin' it."

The doors opened to the top floor, a beige hallway smelling of carpet cleaner and cigar smoke. Meyer walked past door after door, keeping his voice hushed. "High rollers," he said, jabbing a finger at one of the doors. He stopped at one and listened. Michael paused, looking at the polished wood door like it might be the last thing between him and the answers he desperately needed.

"Who's in there?" he asked, prepared for any answer in the world. The first vampire, or Dracula, maybe the devil himself. Meyer took off his hat and smoothed his hair.

"Cyd Charisse."

"Cyd Charisse...? What?"

"Cyd Charisse is in there."

"Cyd Charisse is the...-?"

"Yeah, we're not stopping here. I just think she's a sexy broad." Meyer flashed a smile. He turned and headed down the hallway. Michael wondered if she was actually in there for a second, then followed. They turned a corner and headed straight to a door marked No Admittance.

Meyer deftly unlocked the door, and a fresh wind rushed forth. An iron stairway curled upwards.

"We go up?" Michael asked.

"We go up," nodded Meyer.

Michael stepped out onto the roof, gravel crunching underfoot as he looked at the spiderweb of light arrayed below. Las Vegas. The air up here was clean, and the stars shone in failing competition with the brilliance of Fremont Street to the North. A smell hit him, something acrid and wrong, but ever so faint on the wind. Two men stood on the far end of the long, narrow roof, backs to the light of Fremont so as to render them in silhouette. One stood tall in a long, rumpled coat. The other, lean save a potbelly, hunched like an ape and fidgeted listlessly. Michael couldn't help but notice one of his arms was longer than the other.

" Go ahead," said Meyer, closing the door to the stairs. Michael immediately felt very exposed. He figured that was the point. He walked out toward the two men, hands raised.

" Hello!" he called. "I'm him. I'm... Michael Cage. I've been sending you letters for two years now. I've done everything you've asked. I just want to know about Laura Shepherd. I want to know how she's still alive and ...not aging ...if she's not one of us. I'm willing to comply with whatever you ask, just please... please tell me what's going on?"

The man turned as if he spent his nights up here normally and Michael had interrupted him.

" Michael, Michael, Michael." He waved, and two men pointing rifles at Michael emerged from behind covered air shafts. " Big brother is very disappointed in you."

The first man fired and Michael took it in the ribs. He started to feel the pain ballooning within him, but instinct took over and he switched off the sensation like shutting out a light. He rushed the first gunman, drew his pistol, fired, hitting the second in the face. Michael grabbed the first man's rifle and swung around him, yanking up as hard as he could into the man's throat, breaking his neck before he even knew what was happening. He wheeled to fire at Madison, but Madison was already gone. The fetid stink of the malformed man was eye-watering here, and Michael made the snap decision that there was no way that a misshapen man on a rooftop with his brother could be any good at all. He fired three shots at the freak.

They hit him center mass, and he looked down, blinking as though he'd woken up. Michael hadn't really expected him to go down, but at least for the shots to register. In the light, Michael could see just how hideous he was. He wore a stained white undershirt and grey slacks, thin round glasses, and no shoes. His skin was a pustulent nightmare of lesions and sores, his jaw hung slack, his eyes seemed swollen into a permanent squint. A sore on his cheek opened through to teeth and gums, and his hair grew in sporadic clumps. He hobbled forward, looking at Michael as though up till now they'd been the best of friends, but in the space of three bullets he'd been betrayed.

" Cerberus hurts."

The acrid smell intensified as the man started to grow, releasing a primal burst of pheromones. Michael stepped back, a wave of fear washing over him. The broken man pulled off his glasses and howled. Michael backpedaled, the reality of exactly how truly fucked he was washed over him like high tide.

" Shit. Shit! SHIT!" He ran for the door, but Meyer stood before it, gun drawn. The rising shadow of the broken man shapeshifting in the moonlight fell across him, and he dropped the gun, turned, and bolted down the the stairwell. Michael smelled fur and pus, and he heard Madison's laughter and he hated, he HATED him so much for giving him the satisfaction of seeing him so very scared, but there was a growl and a sound of pads thundering on gravel behind him and oh, Christ how he would have shit his pants were he still able to do so.

The werewolf lunged and Michael dropped flat. It sailed over him and crashed into the stair-shed, mangling it. Michael looked up. He'd never seen a Lupine this close, and this one was hideous. Mangy and brown, it was easily the size of a bear, with long, ropy arms like an ape and canine legs that were thick and broad to support its bulk. Worst of all, though, was its head. Jutting from its canine muzzle on both side were two smaller maws, and it had a third eye on one side of its head, completing the three-faced look. A vestigial claw hung from its chest on one side, and it was coated in weeping sores and pustulent lesions. Its teeth jutted from all three muzzles at horrid angles, foaming and drooling. It shook and snarled and lunged again. Michael rolled, and the monster dug six-inch claws into the gravel to stop itself. Michael got to his feet, looked at the werewolf, the smashed stair-shed, and the at the air shaft. It was his best bet. He bolted for the air shaft, then felt his throat crush and the ground give out from under him. He must have been running at around thirty-five miles per hour when Madison clotheslined him. He landed flat and skidded along the gravel, then stopped, the moon blotted out by Madison over him, a knee in his chest. He flailed, panicked.

" Madison! Madison no! Werewolf! Fucking werewolf gonna...-"

" What, Cerberus?"

The beast loomed, clearly waiting for orders. Michael slowly took it in, shocked.

" It... it listens to you?-AIGH!"

Madison had grasped his arm at the bicep and dislocated it at the shoulder, pressing down to make sure it was broken.

" *He*. He listens to me. He has a name. Tell him your name, big guy."

" Cerberus... name." Its voice was a feverish locomotive made of bears.

The pain was excruciating, and Michael blinked through red tears, flat on his back, unable to free the other arm.

" The Lycanthropes do *not* deal well with atomic testing, do they? I found Cerberus out here a few years back and he responded real well to an understanding friend, didn't you, big guy?"

Cerberus chuffed.

" Whuh... Where... Wheres' La.." Michael stammered.

Madison slapped him.

" She's alive. She was always alive. She was mother's ultimate collateral for you, she's always had such big fucking plans for little brother. She's not gonna die, and she's going to do as mother fucking told her, which is to say she won't get any older and she'll sleep like the fucking dead as soon as the sun leaves the sky every fucking night until the end of time. So fuck you. And fuck her. You will fucking *do as mother says*."

Michael choked, wide-eyed. Taking it in.

" Leucretia said she killed her. She said..."

Madison slammed his head against the gravel.

" I'm asking the questions here, little brother! Me!"

He reached into his coat, drew out a straight razor, and sliced a long, clean line into Michael's cheek just to make sure he knew it was there.

" Where. The. FUCK. Is. Leucretia?"

" I... I don't know!"

" WRONG."

Madison neatly pushed the razor into Michael's right ear and sliced out his tragus, a small flat hunk of cartilage popped free. Michael wailed and almost passed out.

" Where's Leucretia? Where there fuck is our mother?"

Michael tried to contain himself. He'd been hurt bad, but he was wholly unprepared for the unceremonious brutality, a far cry from Leucretia's theatrics. Only once had anything hurt this bad. He knew his body would be able to withstand pain that would kill a human, but his mind was just overloaded. He couldn't even think through the pain. He tried to ignore the damage report his body handed him. Dislocated shoulder. Broken arm. Gunshot wound. FUCKING RAZOR IN MY EAR. Try to hold out.

Madison drew the razor to his lips, allowing a momentary face of disgust when he realized the mistake of tasting blood mixed with earwax.

" You think this is pain? You think this has even fucking begun? I'll slice your cock next."

" Please, no. Please don't."

" Fucking beg me. Beg me, asshole. Say, "Big brother please don't slice my cock.""

Michael sputtered and sobbed, any pretense of resistance long clouded by the pain. He tried to remember what Madison even wanted to know. He'd say anything to make it stop. He blubbered through bloody tears.

" P...Please big brother Madison please don't slice my cock..."

Madison regarded him cooly, and nodded.

" Ok. I'm asking one last time. Where is Leucretia."

" What?"

Madison screamed in rage and rammed the razor up under Michael's upper lip, slicing the thin web of flesh between his gum and his lip, pushing the metal blade up under behind his nose. And quite suddenly, there was no other pain. Only this. Only this, singing agony into his very bones.

" WHERE IS SHE WHERE IS SHE WHERE IS SHE?!!"
" SHE'S DEAD! SHE BURNED IN WHITEHALL!"

Madison ripped the razor free and rolled off of Michael's chest.
Michael pulled his good arm up to cover the flapping, bloody wreck of
his face. Madison stared in shock, and Cerberus put a paw on his arm
to steady him.

" Madison OK?"

" I... I... she's gone..."

Michael lay on his back, focusing all of his blood, knowing he only
had seconds. He surged, time seemed to slow around him and he
rolled to his feet and lunged off the edge of the roof. Madison and
Cerberus blinked at each other, then walked to the edge of the roof.
Looking down, they saw a rope dangling from a single open window
two floors down. He'd escaped.

Madison dropped to one knee and screamed, screamed until the sky
turned pink and his skin blistered and Cerberus gathered him up in his
huge paws and carried him downstairs.

THE TUESDAY AFTER THAT

"We're, uh... Actually, we're damned glad to hear it."
- Thomas Torn, Member of the popular Goth/Industrial band,
"Electric Hellfire Club", upon being told that their music was
being marked as a "warning sign" of Recidivism by the DPBR

It's profoundly surreal being home alone, healthy, and bored as hell at 3 PM on a Tuesday. I sat with a bowl of Lucky Charms in front of the television, watching a black lady in a chef's hat teach a white talk show host (that undoubtedly had her own staff at home) how *to actually cook chitlins*.

Fascinating.

I went back in the kitchen looking to mix up something stronger. One intensely crappy martini later I had again melted into the seat before some other insipid night talk show when a key quietly turned in the lock. Laura swaggered in, stood in front of the TV and put her hands on her hips.

" What are you doing home?"

My gaze darted from the screen to her face. She cocked her head expectantly.

" Well?" She said again.

" Well, what?"

" What are you doing home?"

" I took the day off. I'm feeling shitty."

" Really?"

She leaned in and pressed my forehead.

" You seem okay. Can I get you something?

I shook my head.

70

" You haven't been sick since Coolidge, remember? I'm worried about you."

" Uh. Thanks, no. Not that kind of shitty."

" Well, then, what? Are you depressed?" She seemed overly concerned.

" I dunno. I just... feel... listless, I guess."

She went into the kitchen and I followed.

" Tell me how you feel. Tell me what happened. Tell me what's going on. You're not allowed to pull 'I don't wanna talk about it.' this time, okay? Not with me. "

I nodded, tried to feel something, and touched into a wellspring much closer to the surface than I had expected to find. She jumped as I hit the table. Instead I made something up.

" Granger."

" Still? I thought you were past that."

" It's messing me up, honey. Granger *died*. Forever."

" Part of the deal, honey. Normal people die."

" That wasn't a normal death."

" You said he bled out."

" No! Not normal! That was a murder, god damn it! That shit was supposed to have ended with the cure."

She looked at me as though noticing me for the first time. " Yeah... Go on."

" I mean... I killed people! I killed a lot of people! I fought and bled and risked my life to bring things to some kind of balance, and I watched people die... so many people... for normalcy. For humanity..."

She eased into a seat and took my hand, and I secretly wished she wouldn't. I needed that hand to hit things, to break things. I was absolutely furious.

" No more mysteries, no more violence, no more adventures and conspiracies! I did the work, fought the monsters, and claimed my fucking prize. I breathe, I got the girl, I...-"

She snapped her hand back as though touching something raw. I immediately mentally spun an explanation of how my renewed humanity was the "girl" in question, but we both knew the truth. Her look of concern turned to ice.

" You said you got..? You what?"

" I'm done. I'm done fighting."

I ran my fingers through my hair, and buried my face in my hands.

" You... got what you came for, then." she said, face inscrutable.

I glared at her. We were supposed to be done. Why was she pressing this?

" From where I sat, Laura, you were asleep for fifty fucking years. You don't remember a goddamned thing. You have no idea...-"

" Stop it, Michael. Stop, honestly. Don't."

I squeezed my eyes shut, shook my head, and obeyed.

" This is my fault." She continued. "I shouldn't have pressed you." She sighed. "You don't give a shit about Granger, honey. You miss being invulnerable."

" I just wanted to be normal."

She slammed the door of the freezer which she had seconds before peered into as though it contained answers.

"Jesus Christ, Michael! Shut the fuck up about normal. You're not! *I'm* not! I was fucking cursed for decades, and you fucking drank human blood to survive. Face it! Your fucking training is all about suppression and whatever, and yet you're always mystified when one of you goes recidivist! It's because you all never fucking face the fact that an fundamental aspect of who you are now is a *former fucking vampire!*"

" Blooded."

" Vampire, Michael! You were a vampire for seventy-five years- that's a lifetime! You're a hundred years old and you have black hair, sturdy bones, smooth skin and reliable erections! You are not normal!"

" Don't you think I know that?"

She leaned against the fridge. "There's a difference between knowing and accepting."

I looked up, exasperated. " What do you want from me? I'll try to... I dunno, *accept* it more? Shit. I don't know..."

" No, you won't. Because you're done fighting. I remember you when you were all fire and brimstone. You were a fucking champion.

That part of you fucking died ten years ago, Michael. You died when you started breathing again. "

I watched silently as she went upstairs to work. I snuggled back down onto the couch.

"*Fighting broke out today in the Carpathians, as UN forces were turned away from some of the smaller villages in the East. The Balkan Penninsula also saw renewed violence, and members of the insurrectionist Armata Al Vojvod Noi clashed with local peacekeeping forces outside Bucharest. Islamic Mujahadin have moved against the rebels and the government alike as...-*"

I switched off the TV. Moving slowly, I headed up the stairs into her studio and watched her quietly from the door as she moved with the music and angrily swatted colors at her canvas.

* * * *

Michael Cage held the sleeping woman curled against his side, and considered everything that had led to this moment. From the moment she'd approached him, and stunned him with the opening gambit, "I'm Samantha Canon, and I think maybe you're a Vampire, Michael Cage," to his decision that led here- reversing his principles in almost every way- he had slowly come to the uncomfortable conclusion that he was pretty sure he was in love with her.

She had met him at the airport in Rome. They had been talking for almost a year, and she told him everything about her life, about dealing with her cancer and trying to lead a normal life despite it, and in return he told her everything, confiding everything about his life, about undeath and Laura and his mission and his passion. She bought him a guitar for his birthday, the first birthday present he had received since the '20's.

It made him feel so immensely human.

And here she was. He was awestruck to see her, and although she hustled up to him, her usual girlish spring was gone. He'd come on a stopover for a few days before meeting T'isparigo in Paris, but he told her over the phone that he'd be here to kill a few days and she surprised him by flying out. They "shared" a delicious dish of Polpi in Umido at a quiet late-night trattoria on a terrace overlooking the street. She asked about his broken nose, and he told an embarrassing story. It was almost completely healed, but she had noticed and somewhere inside he appreciated that immensely. When the tall, reed-thin waitress brought the check, Samantha wanted to suggest a return to the hotel, but Michael instead asked where the best place to go dancing would be.

The Piper Club was Rome's most exclusive joint, a converted movie theater that was now the town's loudest discotheque, home to a cover band blasting out Italian versions of American and English hits, much to Michael's amusement. They had danced to "Satisfaction" and "Hang on Sloopy" when the band broke into " For Your Love." Michael launched away from the bar, flanked by dark-haired girls in sweaters and capris, and moved for the floor when he noticed Sam was gone. She was outside.

" What's wrong? I was just getting started in there."

" Fuck you, Michael."

Michael looked down at her, confused. She was crying.

" What... wha?"

" Did you fucking forget?"

She pulled off her hat to reveal her bare scalp, scraps of blonde hair clinging in sad patches. She jabbed a finger at him.

" We talked. I get it. I understand this isn't an alternative and you can't accept creating another killer. I get that. But never forget that I'm dying, Michael. Every day you dance and fuck and live forever, I'm dying. So don't rub it in my fucking face and and expect me to dance with you until... until."

The wave of self-hate that washed over Michael was visible and tangible.

Not a word was said between the two of them as he took her back to his hotel and laid her down and gently made love to her for the first time, never taking his eyes off of her own. And when he climaxed and filled her with blood, those eyes filled with an emotion he mistook for fear before realizing it was love and he wondered if it had been a tremendous mistake.

" What made you change your mind?"

He laid back, spent, and blinked at the ceiling, thinking a long time before he answered.

" I couldn't accept being the one who killed you. Not through violence or inaction. Certainly not on some fucking principle."

She laid back, trying to focus on the same place on the ceiling.

" ...Thank you."

" It's all different, now. You have forever starting tonight. That hazy pink over Porta Pia was your last sunset. Forever."

" ... How perfect is that, then?"

" Don't trivialize this, Samantha. You're going to kill people. Innocent people. You'll take up space that should be occupied by new people, reverse the natural cycle. Do good. Make it worthwhile that you have been given this."

She blinked.

" I won't let you down."

" You should meet T'isparigo. I'm meeting him in Paris in a few days."

" Who is that?"

" He's the oldest vampire I've ever met. Wise, wise like you would imagine a priest or shaman should be. Jasmine introduced me to him in Djakarta back in the 50's."

" Djakarta...?"

" You'll travel, Samantha. The world will be yours."

" I'm broke. I didn't even buy a return ticket. I had planned to die here."

Michael thought about that, but it was too big to address, so he chose to ignore it.

" You won't be for too long. I'll show you how to invest."

" Thank you."

" Don't mention it."

Samantha tried to determine what part of the ceiling Michael was looking at. For his part, Michael was quite certain he was looking through it.

" That was my last meal, right? Of real food?"

" Yeah. I'll get someone for you to eat tomorrow night. And you won't kill them. I'm going to make sure of that."

" What was your ... Maker like?"

Michael shook his head quietly, indicating that that would under no circumstances ever be a topic of conversation here. He never felt quite so in control, quite so much the elder vampire, so ancient and possessed of forbidden knowledge. He had wanted to enjoy it more, but every word seemed to clarify for him just how bad the situation had the potential to become. He wanted to not seem so distant with her, so preoccupied, but it took everything he had to shield her from the waves of nauseous regret he was feeling.

" Thank you, Michael."

" Don't thank me. Please."

" You saved my life."

" No. You're dead now. I killed you. You're about to become sicker than you have ever been. You're about to feel pain like you couldn't have known."

She got up on her elbows as if to direct his attention to her chemo-wracked scalp. He gave her a look to clarify that he stood by exactly what he had said. She lay back down.

" I know everything you told me still holds. I don't care. I love you, Michael Cage. I love you and I always will. And tonight, at least, you're mine."

She placed her head on his chest and closed her eyes.

Michael looked at her. He wondered exactly how important his plans really were? Could he drop everything and run away with this woman? Why hadn't he mentioned Laura? It's not like they both didn't know. What would T'isparigo say to him? How could he do to anyone what Leucretia had done to him?

But what if just this moment everything changed and he became a vampire in love with his creation? What if together they traveled Europe and loved each other and enjoyed this facsimile of life as a series on unstructured moments stretching on into infinity....

No.

He could no sooner run away from his plan than he could run away from the sky. Michael got to his feet and hung a thick blanket over one window, crossed to the door and hung out the Do Not Disturb sign.

He moved to the far side of the room and leaned against the window, bathed in the orange electric light from the street below. Across from him, a sign in front of a church assured him, in Italian, that only Jesus can save souls. He stared for a long time before a sound from the bed startled him.

Samantha's eyes squeezed tight and she twitched as the first twinges of pain issued up from her gut. She choked, but did not wake. Michael went to the bathroom and gently wet a washcloth with cool water to dab at her searing brow as she began to wretch and cough and choke up everything that had once made her biologically human.

It was the beginning of an impossibly long night.

* * * *

Noticing me, she looked over and smiled, wiping her face on her ratty sleeve.

I walked to her and took her hand, gently as though asking her to dance. She smiled and offered it. Gathering her to me, I kissed her neck and smelled her hair and scooped her up, carried her to the table, and laid her down on it. She sighed quietly, pulling down her jeans and leaning back on her elbows.

" Normal, eh?"

" Reliable." I countered.

I took a knee like a supplicant knight between her thighs and buried my face in her thatch, taking in everything I could. She watched me, smiling a coy half grin as she played with me hair.

" Do you still feel my pulse when you do that?"

I nodded.

" So attuned to the blood, Michael. Do you know if I'm lying when you're down there? Like my heart rate might change?"

" I don't know. Start telling lies."

" I am a world famous artist."

I looked up but didn't stop. I pushed in, trying to get a sense of change in the flushed skin all around me. She giggled and carried on. " Blue is my favorite color."

I shook my head. " Now tell the truth," I mumbled.

" Orange is my favorite color."

I nodded.

"Crocodiles eat only salad. You spent two years in Kansas. Uhhnn.... The sky is green. We are less than ten miles from Manhattan island. Oh, uh... Our house is haunted. I ... wrote a book about patterns. The dog is barking. I love what you're doing."

I looked up and her eyes caught mine, and her expression went from whimsy to contemplative, like a scientist watching a subject react to new stimuli.

" ... I love *you*." she said, never taking her eyes off mine, challenging me to determine the truth.

End of Book 2

To Be Continued in...

BOOK TWO: A FAMILIAR GROTESQUE